BULLET LEASE

D. B. Newton

D1545691

Chivers Press • G.K. Hall & Co.
Bath, England   Thorndike, Maine USA

This Large Print edition is published by Chivers Press, England, and by G.K. Hall & Co., USA.

Published in 2000 in the U.K. by arrangement with the author c/o Golden West Literary Agency.

Published in 2000 in the U.S. by arrangement with Golden West Literary Agency.

U.K. Hardcover   ISBN 0-7540-4131-X   (Chivers Large Print)
U.K. Softcover   ISBN 0-7540-4132-8   (Camden Large Print)
U.S. Softcover   ISBN 0-7838-9015-X   (Nightingale Series Edition)

F
n̲eet
LT

The text of this Large Print edition is unabridged.
Other aspects of the book may vary from the original edition.

Set in 16 pt. New Times Roman.

Printed in Great Britain on acid-free paper.

British Library Cataloguing in Publication Data available

Library of Congress Cataloging-in-Publication Data

   Newton, D. B. (Dwight Bennett), 1916–
      Bullet lease : a Western novel / by D.B. Newton.
         p. cm.
      ISBN 0-7838-9015-X (lg. print : sc : alk. paper)
      1. Large type books. I. Title.
   PS3527.E9178 B8 2000
   813'.52—dc21

99–462294

BULLET LEASE

CHAPTER ONE

It must have been close to three in the morning when Branch Kindred reached Anchor headquarters. He rode in quietly, with the tired stockinged roan stumbling under him and his own spare figure slumped in the leather. He had covered a far distance since dawn, completing his two-day survey of the range that the coming of spring had opened up. He was overdue for bed.

On the whole, he brought back a satisfactory report. Old snow still clogged the timbered hills, so it would be some time before beef stock could be taken to the higher meadows; but that snow promised a good hold-back of drainage for the months ahead. Most important of all, the grass was already pushing up, rich and heavy on the Dumont Lease. There, the drifts were mostly gone, and Sam Hazen would be glad to know he could begin moving in his cattle as quickly as it was gathered and branded.

Anchor slept, the main house and bunkshack and other buildings dark and completely silent. The only light was a lantern hanging from a post in front of the barn. Night wind moaned around the eaves and the lantern swayed, rocking its circle of yellow light across the ground and the barn's cavernous doorway;

still, it was enough to help Kindred with the work of unsaddling and turning his roan into the night corral, where it would find feed and water.

He spread his sweated blanket. Afterward, blowing the barn lantern, he stood for a moment in the chill, smelling a hint of spring in the air and seeing the evidence of roundup activity. A good ranch, this one, with a stern but fair boss in old Sam Hazen. Branch Kindred nodded in satisfaction, telling himself again he was lucky to be a part of it—lucky, starting from nothing, to have reached the status of foreman of such an outfit when he had, at the age of twenty-nine. Five years on the job, he tallied, and shook his head a little as he reckoned the passing of time.

Well, you couldn't ask the years to stand still for you, or hold on to the vigor of youth forever. Tonight, after almost twenty steady hours in the saddle, Branch Kindred felt as old as Sam Hazen himself. But he was still young enough that he knew a few hours' sleep could bring him bounding back.

He picked up his saddle and toted it across the yard, to the two-room house that was his by virtue of his position as Anchor foreman. He turned in and slept soundly.

Next morning he woke late, for him. Sunlight, clearing the high angle of the barn roof, struck through the dusty window and fell across his face as he lay in the old iron bed.

Kindred crooked an arm to shield his eyes and listened to the familiar sounds of a stirring ranch, feeling the warmth of the sun begin to lift the edges of the chill from the room. He wasn't a man in the habit of spending much time like this, however, and shortly he threw off the blankets. The old springs groaned under him as he levered himself up and reached for boots and shirt and trousers.

A mirror propped on nails driven in the wall showed him his reflection—the rather spare features, the stubborn jaw, the eyes so used to squinting into strong sunlight that they had taken on something of a perpetual scowl. It was a pleasant enough face, for all that, the eyes being mildly blue, the mouth generous; but Kindred was not much given to thinking about his appearance. He ran a hand through wiry back hair, down across the dark beard stubble that clouded his cheeks. He could use a shave, he decided, and taking the battered tin basin from the washstand he walked out of the house and across to the cook-shack, to beg some hot water.

Hazen's eight-man crew was still at breakfast. A clatter of silverware and heavy china and a racket of talk met Kindred as he came through warm sunshine and up the two slab steps to the door. Heads lifted when the door opened. At once, the voices ceased. In a sudden stillness, Branch Kindred knew that something was afoot.

3

Big Ed Farrar was the first to speak. 'Hell, we didn't know you was here, Branch! You just get in?'

'Last night.'

'See the boss?'

'Why, no. I rode in late. The whole place was asleep. Anything wrong?' Kindred scanned the faces lining the long trestle table, where steam rose from coffee pot and from platters loaded with eggs and bacon and pan-fried spuds. 'Something happened while I was out?'

The crew exchanged looks. Farrar, the spokesman, rubbed a fist across his stubby mustache. 'It has, for a fact,' he said. 'The old man's son—'

'Earl Hazen?' Astonishment slacked Kindred's jaw. 'Are you telling me Sam's had word, after all this time?'

'More than that, Branch. He's here!'

'Here, at Anchor?'

Farrar nodded. 'Come yesterday afternoon. just dropped out of nowhere, without even a hint.'

A long breath slowly left Kindred's lungs.

'He's up at the house,' Farrar went on. 'In his old room, that I guess Sam's had waitin' for him all these eighteen years—or however long it is he's been gone.'

'There was another gent with him,' a hand named Tom Grady offered. 'Called himself Roth, or some such. But he went back to town.

4

Sounded to us like they had a business deal of some kind.'

Kindred shook free of his first astonishment, and discovered that he still held the tin basin forgotten in one hand. As he laid it down he noticed the vacant chair at the end of the table and asked, 'Isn't Sam up?'

'No sign yet,' the cook answered. 'How about when you fixed the fire, Grady?' But the puncher shook his head.

On an impulse, Kindred turned back to the door. His hand was on the china knob when Ed Farrar said, 'What do you want us to do about Judy, Branch? She's still visiting over at Montrose. She ought to know about her paw being home. You want one of us should go into town and send a wire?'

Kindred hesitated, then shook his head. 'I'll let you know,' he said. 'After I've talked with Sam.'

Crossing the working area of the ranch yard to where Sam Hazen's house stood inside its own picket fence, he was still a little stunned by what he'd heard. He also felt a vague uneasiness. Earl Hazen's return was bound of course to have consequences. For one thing, he supposed it would almost certainly mean some difference in his own status as foreman of Anchor, though he wasn't particularly worried about that. He would be dealt with justly, for his five years in the job. He knew he could count on Sam.

But there were strange angles that had never been explained, concerning the son who had been gone for so many years—gone so long, in fact, that no member of Anchor's present crew had ever even seen him. Kindred had more or less supposed he must be dead. He was sure Judy Hazen felt the same way, and he found himself thinking of the shock in store for Judy, when she learned that the father who'd walked out of her life when she was less than a year old had suddenly turned up, alive, and was right now here in her grandfather's house.

Kindred opened the gate and walked up the path, between flower beds that lay dark and fallow from the winter just past. The tall old house, with its high-pitched roof and the scrollwork at the gables, stood silent in a new day. Morning sun burnished the narrow windows that reached almost from floors to high ceilings. Smoke from the fire young Grady had built in the Franklin stove poured out of the chimney.

On the veranda Kindred paused. He heard nothing but the lonely whistle of a meadowlark somewhere in the wired pasture beyond the house. He opened the door and entered.

A blast of heat met him, a rush and roar of flames in the red hot pipe of the big space heater standing in a corner of the living room. Quickly he turned the damper. The roaring ceased, the chimney popping as it began to

6

cool. Heat still billowed strongly into the room from the fire that had nearly got out of hand. Frowning, Kindred looked at the closed door of old Sam's bedroom, and at that other door to the hall and the back part of the house, and at the staircase leading up to the second floor. And then a sound from the corner by the front window made him turn.

The round center table with its lamp masked that corner, so that he hadn't noticed Sam Hazen. The old cowman sat in his favorite rocker. Sam had pulled a bathrobe around himself and thrust his bare feet into carpet slippers. His chin was on his breast, and his deep-sunk eyes regarded his foreman from beneath shaggy brows. Seeing him like that gave Kindred an odd start. It made him realize for the first time, clearly, just how much Sam had fallen off—how little he resembled the husky, saddle-tough rancher Branch Kindred had first signed on with as a common hand, nine years ago.

True, since Kindred became foreman his boss had taken less and less of an active role in managing Anchor; but until this moment Kindred had failed to realize the slackness that had come into his wiry frame. He looked every day of his seventy years, right now, and the sight of him, crumpled there in the chair while the old stove crackled and roared dangerously, made Kindred take a step toward him, feeling a kind of alarm.

But Sam Hazen was the first to speak. 'Hello, Branch,' he said, in a voice that sounded oddly unlike his. 'Back already? How do things look?'

'Are you all right, Sam?'

Sam Hazen lifted his hand in an impatient gesture. 'Tell me about the grass!' he said. 'How's the range shaping up? What kind of a season is it going to be?'

'It looks pretty good, Sam.'

Not a word about the return of the missing son! Sam's first and last interest must always be for Anchor, and for the welfare of this ranch he'd devoted his life to. So Kindred proceeded to satisfy him, giving his report on the promise of good grass and melt water, and particularly on the shape-up of the vital Dumont Lease. Sam listened, nodding a little, and when his foreman finished he gave a grunt of satisfaction.

'Good—good!' he said. 'Then we'll go right ahead with the spring gather.'

'Sure, Sam.'

Kindred made no move to leave. He couldn't get over this. The waxen face, the sunken cheeks, the nose thinned down to a bony ridge by the long erosion of time . . . He cleared his throat uncertainly. 'Sam, the boys tell me—'

The slam of a door overhead interrupted him. Footsteps tramped along the upper hall. The old man's head and eyes followed the

8

sound. 'They told you about this?' Kindred nodded. Slowly he turned toward the stairs.

He saw a pair of town shoes, then gray trouser-legs and a suitcoat sleeve and a hand trailing the bannister. Earl Hazen came down the steps, into the living room. Kindred had no idea what to expect, but what walked in was a man of about forty, give or take a year or two; a man who wore his sack suit and string tie with no particular air of distinction, whose skin was pale, who looked soft. His hair, worn rather long, was thinning at the temples, yet it was the same fine, light hair that he had bequeathed to his daughter Judy.

Sam's hair must have been like that at one time. But any other resemblance between father and son lay buried so deep under the soft, fatty flesh of Earl Hazen's face that you had to dig to find it. A sullen man, Kindred thought. Those heavily-lidded eyes would smolder dully in anger.

Earl Hazen paused at the foot of the stairs. He looked around, and saw his father in the rocker by the window. At once his mouth drew down hard. He took a couple of purposeful strides, noticed the third party in the room, and stopped abruptly.

Sam Hazen roused himself to mumble, 'My foreman, Branch Kindred. This is my son, Earl.'

They looked at each other for a long moment, a mutual sizing up. Neither spoke.

9

Abruptly, Earl Hazen swung again to his father. His voice held an angry rasp. It was exactly as though he picked up the thread of an interrupted argument.

'Dad, I can tell you now we're not through with this business. It's an opportunity and I'm damned if I let you pass it up.'

Sam raised a hand in mild protest. 'All right, Earl,' he said, and he sounded infinitely tired. 'We'll discuss it later.'

'Not later!' The son's soft hands knotted. He took another step that brought him to a stand above the old man in the chair. 'That's exactly what you said last night—when you walked into your room and locked the door on me! I tell you, if we waste any time over this proposition Roth isn't going to wait. He'll be gone and his money with him—and it's a price we won't be offered every day in the year!'

Kindred winced, not at the talk of selling Anchor, but at Sam Hazen's failure to react. He knew where the old rancher's love lay. Why, only a year ago the mere suggestion would have brought Sam to his feet, fighting mad. But Sam merely rocked his head against the back of the chair and repeated, 'Later, Earl. Please!'

'Damn it,' Earl Hazen shouted. 'I tell you—'

Kindred found his own voice, then. 'Didn't you hear him?'

For a moment, Earl Hazen stood stock still. Then, very slowly, he turned toward Branch

10

Kindred. His lips scarcely moved as he asked, 'You said something?'

'Sam did,' Kindred answered flatly. 'He said he wanted to talk some other time about this thing, whatever it is.'

'And what business is it of yours?'

Kindred fought down the anger the man's tone raised in him. 'None, I reckon. Just the same, I think you better do what the boss says—and he says let it ride for now!' He jerked his head toward the door. 'Why don't you go down to the cookshack, get yourself some breakfast or something?'

Color started to flow up through Earl Hazen's face. It ebbed, leaving his mouth tight and white at the corners. Kindred expected an argument. Instead Earl Hazen strode to the door and flung it open. He turned there, and he said, 'What was your name again?'

Kindred told him. Hazen nodded, lips moving faintly as though memorizing it, linking it past forgetting with the tall and saddle-whipped figure of the Anchor foreman. Then with a toss of the head and an angry swing of his shoulders he strode on, across the veranda and down the steps. He left the door wide open.

Face expressionless, Kindred watched Earl Hazen move down the path, jerk the gate open and walk toward the kitchen shack. After that he hushed the door shut.

'Sorry, Sam,' he said. 'I didn't intend to butt

11

into a family matter.'

Sam nodded dully. Again Kindred wondered at the strange apathy that seemed to rest on him. He walked over and stood frowning down at Sam's shaggy white head. 'Sounded to me like he was talking about selling Anchor to this fellow Roth, whoever he is. It's none of my affair, of course—'

'But you're surprised I'd sit here and let him make such talk?' The old head lifted, and Kindred saw tears in Hazen's eyes and a mouth shaped by tragedy. 'I couldn't help myself, Branch. Pull over a chair. I got—I got something to tell you.'

Kindred hauled over one of the stiff chairs from beside the table. Hazen's voice was so unsteady and faint that he had to lean close to be sure he caught the words.

'I've had a stroke, Branch.'

Kindred blinked and sat there, not comprehending. 'You—*what*?' he said finally. 'But how do you know?'

'It already happened to me once. Three years back, just before I stopped taking much of an active part in running the ranch.'

Kindred pulled himself together. 'I guess maybe I remember,' he said slowly. 'You were in bed for awhile—' An attack of pleurisy, the doctor had called it. And when he got up again, Sam had seemed a strangely altered man, with the vigor gone from him. But Kindred, feeling the weight of suddenly

12

increased responsibility, had had little time to think about this change. He said, 'Why did you keep it a secret?'

'Didn't want to scare Judy,' Sam Hazen said. 'The doc told me if I took care of myself it might never happen again. But if there ever was a second attack, the third could come at any time—and that would be the one.'

'You sure you couldn't be mistaken?'

'About last night?' Sam Hazen shrugged. 'I guess I ought to know the symptoms. It wasn't much of a stroke a light one. But I woke up to find my whole left side feeling numb, and something wrong with my speech. And my mind won't track, Branch. No, there's no doubt at all.

He passed his hand vaguely across his forehead. 'I finally got on my feet, and I could walk. I made it as far as this chair. But then the juice seemed to run out of me.

'Too much excitement,' he went on, in that dull, thick voice that had puzzled Kindred. 'I know that's what brought it on. The boy coming home, and bringing that stranger with him, and all the wrangle over him wanting to sell Anchor.'

Kindred started to his feet. 'Hell! I better get someone off for town, Sam, and have the doctor out here.'

'That can wait a minute, Branch. I want to talk.'

'All right,' Kindred said, and settled back

13

knowing that anxiety must be showing in his face.

The veined hand came groping toward him. It settled on his wrist in a grip that lacked strength. 'Branch, I'm going to have to lean on you now—lean like I never done before. Earl will sell this spread in a minute if he gets a chance. We've got to stop him.'

'He's your own son,' Kindred reminded him.

Hazen made a negative gesture. 'So much the worse for Anchor,' he said bitterly. 'I've never told you about him, have I? About the time he left home?'

'No.'

'It's something I've never discussed with anyone, Branch.'

Hazen's glance wandered to the window, but he probably saw nothing of the bright morning outside. 'My own fault, I guess it was,' he said after a moment. 'Earl was my only son and after his mother died I spoiled him. He grew up selfish and irresponsible. I never could get him to take an interest in the ranch. All he had in mind to do was get away—away from Colorado, back East where there were more people and what he called something going on.' He sighed. 'Then one time, he met a girl who worked in a hashhouse over in Gunnison. He married her and brought her here.'

'That was Judy's mother?'

Sam nodded. 'A nice enough girl. I hoped she might help to settle him. But after a year

14

she died, at the time Judy was born. I think in his own way Earl must really have loved her. He started drinking heavy—and him scarcely more than a kid even then. Just turned twenty-one . . .'

The voice trailed off, as Sam drifted back into memories that were too humiliating and painful to talk about easily. Kindred waited. 'And then?' he prompted gently.

The old man lifted a hand, examined it, grimaced, let it drop again. 'I thought a change of scene might help—some responsibility to shoulder. Having a motherless daughter on his hands didn't seem to be enough. Earl scarcely even noticed Judy. So when she was maybe six months old I sent him off to Chicago with a beef shipment. He'd been there before, of course, with me. He knew the town and the cattle dealers. He knew this sale was important because the Dumont section had gone on the market and I was anxious to bid it in.'

Kindred's breath was shallow in his throat. 'But he never came back?'

'He never came back. It was the chance he'd been lookin' for, I guess. He took the beef money and went after some of that excitement he'd been wanting, and that was the last I heard of him. I covered up for him, though losing the money just then nearly ruined me. Bill Marshall bought in the Dumont land. Luckily he was a friend of mine and he let me have it on lease. Otherwise I don't know what

15

Anchor would have been doing, these eighteen years.

Kindred heard himself saying slowly, 'What kind of nerve would it take, to come back—now—after doing a thing like that?'

'I'd thought time might have changed him, matured him some.' Sam shook his head. 'But it didn't take me long to know that it hasn't.'

'Where's he been all this time? What's he been up to?'

'Who knows? Helling around, I gather. Wasting his life. And now he's come across this man Roth. Roth claims he has cash and wants to buy land here on the west slope. That's the only reason he's bothered to come back. And I'm scared, Branch.'

Sam Hazen's trembling hand reaching again for his foreman's arm. 'If anything happens to me now it'll be the end of Anchor. I know that, and it ain't what I've gone and given my life for. Judy loves this ranch, the way I do. She's got to have it for her own.' His voice rose, cracked. 'We can't let that no-good sell it out from under her!'

Branch said, 'Your will's made, isn't it, Sam?'

The old head rocked wearily against the padded chair back. 'Long ago. I put this ranch in trust for Judy till she's of age, and I named you administrator. But, how do I know it will stick? This is Judy's own father we're dealing with—my own son. He told me last night, in so

16

many words, that if I tried to cut him out he'd go before the court and demand that the will be set aside, and have himself named executor. You know what that would mean.'

'I guess I do,' Kindred said grimly.

'All these years I've been bucking Judge Gore's political hold on this county. He'd jump at any chance to get even—especially if Earl was to make it worth his while to have Anchor turned over to him.'

'You really think Earl would go that far?'

'That's the kind he is, Branch—heedless and completely selfish. To stop him I'd have to reopen that business eighteen years ago, and brand him for a thief. I can't, for Judy's sake. It'll be a fight, whatever happens, and it kills me to think of me gone and Judy facing it alone, without anyone to lean on. Branch—' Sam's troubled eyes seemed to be pleading now. 'It would help to ease my mind a hell of a lot if—' He hesitated over the words, and then blurted them out. 'Well, had you ever thought of—marrying Judy?'

'Sam, you don't know what you're saying!'

'She thinks a lot of you.'

'But not that way. Why, I'm half again her age.'

Sam Hazen studied him for a long time. 'I guess I understand,' Sam said finally, and sadly. 'It's still Gwen Marshall with you, ain't it?'

Kindred felt the tightening in his throat.

'What would you know about me and Gwen?'

Hazen made a small gesture. 'Nothing—except what I sort of guessed, the time she and Bill was married. It hit you pretty hard.'

'She married a man who had more to offer than I did,' Kindred said in a flat tone. 'That was her privilege. And it's got nothing to do with what we were talking about.'

'Sure,' Sam said. 'Of course. What I suggested—you and Judy—you're right. It was only a desperate old man's foolish notion that never would have worked. But you will watch out for Judy? Promise me that, Branch.'

'Certainly I promise. Only you aren't going to die, Sam.'

'It could happen any time,' the rancher said doggedly.

'Right now there's one thing I do want you to do for me, though, Branch. Get word to Montrose and bring Judy home. I want her with me. I can't sit around waiting for that third stroke to hit me—knowing I might never see my girl again.'

'All right, Sam. I'll send a wire.'

He was at the door when Sam called after him. 'But mind you don't scare her. She ain't to know about this. Let her think it's because her paw's come back that you're fetchin' her home. Understand?'

Kindred nodded, and went out of the house.

CHAPTER TWO

The chill freshness of spring felt good, after the parched heat of the living room. He stood a moment letting the ground wind blow moistly against him and catching the welcome scent of growing things that it carried across the hills. Then he walked toward the cookshack.

Most of the men had finished breakfast and were setting about the routine of a busy morning. He saw nothing of Earl Hazen. He met Ed Farrar and ordered him to saddle a horse and head for town and get the doctor.

'The doc!' Farrar echoed. 'What's up? Something wrong with Sam?'

'His dinner didn't set right, I guess. Nothing serious.'

'Glad it ain't,' Farrar said. 'Did you meet the son? What did you think of him?'

Kindred was in no mood to talk. He shrugged, and the cowpuncher ambled toward the corral to saddle up. Kindred got the basin of hot water the cook had poured for him and carried it, steaming, to his own quarters.

He was standing at the battered wash stand in his bedroom, scraping at his lathered face with a long-shanked razor, when he heard the outer door open. 'Yeah?' he called, and getting no answer he turned with razor still poised.

19

Earl Hazen came into the connecting door, and put his shoulder against the edge of it. Kindred regarded him with surprise and ill-concealed hostility. Slowly he finished the stroke of the blade. He dipped it into the water. The faint hiss of the lather dissolving was an audible sound.

'Something I can do for you?' Kindred asked.

'No,' Hazen said. 'Except to talk. I'm afraid we didn't hit it off very well up at the house. My fault, Kindred. I flew off the handle. I'm sorry.'

Kindred tried to read what lay behind the heavy-lidded blue eyes. Failing, he turned back to the mirror. 'Forget it,' he said, and began another stroke with the blade.

'You seem to be popular with the crew,' Earl Hazen went on. 'A good cowman—a good foreman.'

The razor paused. 'So you've been asking the boys about me?'

'Certainly! I thought it was my business to know just what kind of man my father'd had in here, to run things for him. I'm pleased to learn that you've apparently done a good job. He seems to lean on you pretty hard. I'm grateful to you.'

'Thanks,' Kindred said drily. He tilted his chin, to get at the elusive patches of bristle along his corded throat.

'I'm afraid I've been a disappointment,' he

20

heard Earl Hazen saying. 'But there's things about a man he has no power to change. This kind of life wasn't for me. It never was. I just couldn't have stuck it out. And when Rose— when my wife died, I knew I had to get away.' He cleared his throat as if embarrassed. 'You know what I did, I suppose. I'm not proud of it. I guess, if you care to put it that way, I've wasted my life. I honestly envy a man like you, Kindred—a man who can pick out his place, find his job to do and stick to it. I wish I'd had some of what you've got.'

Was this all empty flattery, or was a little of it sincere? Kindred wondered about it as he laid down his razor, rinsed the rest of the lather from his face and reached dripping for a towel. Whatever had come over this man, his tone had changed since their first meeting at the house. Kindred studied the sullen blue eyes, the face that was a blurred copy of old Sam's—a face softened by too long indulgence, by too rich food, by careless and undirected years. He took his shirt off a knob of the bed and drew it on. He shoved the tails home and began to work at the buttons.

He said, 'Sam tells me you've got a buyer lined up. Fellow named Roth. Who is he?'

'Croyden Roth, from New Mexico. At least his main operation is there. He's a man with a good many irons in the fire. I met him in Kansas City. Roth was looking for additional range and I happened to tell him something

21

about this part of western Colorado, and he got interested. One thing led to another. We ended by taking the train west for a look.'

'Merely on the strength of what you were able to tell him?' Kindred frowned skeptically. 'I'd have thought things would be considerably changed in eighteen years.'

'Naturally,' Hazen agreed. 'And the biggest change has been in my father.' He shook his head, his face taking on sober lines. 'You know, Kindred, I was shocked when I saw him. It never occurred to me that he would look so old. And sick! Did you notice, this morning?' He sighed. 'Well, anyway, that's the reason I want to ask your help.'

Kindred raised an eyebrow. '*My* help?'

'He's got to sell this place! I know how he feels about it, but it's just too big a load for him to carry any longer. For his own good, he's got to be persuaded it's time he dropped the burden. Roth liked the property, Kindred. He'll pay a good price.'

Kindred felt a cold distaste settle, rock-hard, inside him. He turned and looked fully at Earl Hazen. He didn't try to withhold the scorn from his voice as he said, 'Out of curiosity, how much commission does Roth pay you on the sale?'

An indrawn breath whistled sharply between Hazen's teeth. He said, 'Why, damn you!' and came lunging away from the door.

A fist struck at Kindred. It was a clumsy

22

blow, coming in so slow that Kindred didn't even need to duck. He simply raised his own rope-hard hand, caught the wrist and jerked it sideward, flinging Hazen against the wall with a force that shook it.

The man was nearly Kindred's size but Kindred pinned him easily. Earl Hazen glared at him furiously. His chest heaved within the sack coat, and his face was stained with angry color. Kindred released the imprisoned arm and stepped back.

'You don't fool me much,' he said, harshly. 'All that tender concern about old Sam's wellbeing is phony and I know it. You stole money from him—your own father. You pulled out when he needed you most and left your child for him to raise any way he could. You broke his heart. And now, because you see a chance to put some money in your worthless pocket, you have the brazen nerve to come back here and try to force him to sell Anchor. And cheat Judy out of her birthright!'

'Well, go right ahead. Maybe you can do the trick, and maybe you can't—you and this stranger you've dragged out here with you. But get one thing straight, mister. All the smooth talk you care to make won't get you any help from me!'

By the time he finished, the color had drained from Earl Hazen's face, leaving it putty colored. A nervous tic was fluttering in the puckered flesh below one glaring eye. He

23

straightened a little, his back still against the wall.

'You're going to be sorry,' he promised in a half whisper. 'You'll wish you'd never talked this way to me.'

'I'm not interested in threats, either,' Branch Kindred said. 'Now get out of my house.'

He watched Earl Hazen go.

He went into the other room to get his hat and brush jacket. Anger walked with him as he left for work, slamming the door of the little house behind him—and anger the knowledge that he hadn't heard the last of that scene.

*   *   *

Croyden Roth descended to the lobby of the hotel in Rock River. He felt the sway of the broad and creaking staircase, he noticed a large brown stain that rain leakage had left on the wallpaper, and he thought with amused contempt of the many such fifth-rate hotels he'd stayed in. But there had been better ones, too—in San Francisco, in Denver and Chicago and St. Louis and even farther afield. He could always put up with discomfort and inconvenience when—as now—it was a matter of business necessity.

The desk clerk bobbed a greeting, ducking his chin into his yellowed celluloid collar. 'Good morning, Mr. Roth. A fine day! I hope you slept real comfortable.'

'Well, enough, thank you.' This was strictly true. A lumpy mattress or a rat gnawing in the wall could never be allowed to spoil his night; neither could the nagging pressure of a move miscalculated, a plan gone awry. As far as yesterday's unsatisfactory visit at Anchor was concerned, Roth had always been able to push such matters into some pigeonhole in his brain, where they could wait until he was full of fresh ideas again, and ready to attend to them.

'Serving breakfast in the dining room, Mr. Roth.'

He nodded absently, but strolled across the dingy lobby and out upon the veranda. There he stood in the sun and measured the day ahead.

The town matched the hotel, he thought; he had been in a hundred like it. He took out a leather cigar holder, chose one of the expensive brand he favored and placed it unlighted between firm, clean-shaven lips. He was not a tall man, this Croyden Roth, but very solid in an unobtrusive, non-bulgy sort of way. A casual stranger, noticing the cut of Roth's expensive clothing, was apt to ticket him for the usual, soft-living business man and miss the heavy bone structure and the smooth muscle hidden underneath. Croyden Roth had come up through a tough school but he had sluffed most of the marks of it. This deceived

25

people and he found the fact amusing.

An unprepossessing red barn of a building, which was actually the town bank, took and held his interest. As he contemplated its closed doors and blank windows, speculatively, a man with a county sheriff's star on his coat lapel came along the sidewalk. This, he had learned last evening, was Cliff Johnson—a jovial, vacant-eyed man. At sight of the well-dressed figure on the porch Johnson grinned and his finger touched his hatbrim in a salute. 'Morning, Mr. Roth. Fine day, ain't it? Be summer before we know.'

'Good morning, Sheriff.'

As the officer moved on, Roth considered how the prices of men varied. Some came cheap, some more dearly—but there was always a price, if you raised the ante far enough. It was poor business, on the other hand, to offer more than was strictly necessary; and Roth prided himself on his ability to gauge a man to the nicest shading. For Sheriff Johnson, now, the price had been low indeed—a few flattering words and a cigar from the leather case. For no more investment than this, he had won not only the officer's fawning admiration but—what was more important—an interesting hour's talk in the jail office, after his return from Anchor.

On the wall there had been an enlarged map of the county. Roth's probing questions, and the lawman's natural garrulity, had gained

26

Roth the commodity he most greatly needed at this stage of the game—information. He had succeeded so well that, although he'd actually seen very little as yet of this foothill graze, he held a very thorough mental picture of its possibilities. The wall map itself was imprinted in his mind with all the vividness of a photograph.

An interesting country, he mused as he put the unlighted cigar away and turned back into the hotel. Worth looking into. Croyden Roth wasn't thinking in terms of scenery, however. The drama of towering mountain faces, the beauty of cedar brakes and aspen and dark timber and bunch grass meadows, did not interest him. The magic of springtime in Colorado left him unmoved. All Croyden Roth wanted out of any country was wealth and power.

The hotel dining room held three small tables covered with red checkered gingham, and cane-seated chairs that felt greasy to the touch. Roth sat by the window and worked methodically at his lumpy potatoes and half-cooked eggs; he had a stomach of iron and if good food wasn't available he could eat bad. Indifferent now to what he happened to be putting in his stomach, he summed up the problem as he saw it.

Anchor held the key. The map showed that plainly. In this land the balance of summer and winter range was all-important; and Anchor, by its location, owned an advantage over its half-dozen neighbors that could—in the hands of a man other than Sam Hazen—mean eventual control. But his first encounter with the old man convinced Roth that Earl Hazen was an even bigger fool than he had judged him. Old Sam was not going to sell his ranch—not without harder pressure than his son could ever put on him. And the urgency which pressed on Roth gave him little time for delay.

By the time he left the hotel, the bank's window shades had been run up and the door stood open for business. He strolled across the rutted street, that still had some of the iron of unthawed earth beneath its surface coating of wheel-raised dust, and entered the gloomy building

A few minutes closeted with Frank Chaffee, who was Red Rock's bald and potbellied banker, convinced Roth that this man had an even lower selling price than the sheriff. He was right. All it took was a single look at the figures on the bank draft Roth drew from his pocket. He let Chaffee's watery eyes go round with greed, behind their thick, rimless spectacles, and then he put the draft away again.

'If I can find the right property,' he said, 'I intend to transfer part of my operations and cash resources up here. I have a crew and a thousand head of beef on the trail already, from New Mexico.'

Chaffee's attention never left the pocket where the paper had vanished. He touched tongue to his lips and said, 'We'll be happy to have your account, Mr. Roth. Meanwhile, if you like, we'd be only too glad to let you place that draft in the vault, for safe keeping.'

'Not necessary,' Roth said, and got to his feet. 'I'm just looking around, getting acquainted. You have a fine town here—a prosperous looking country. Would you perhaps be agreeable to joining me at the hotel bar for a little drink?'

'Why, thank you,' the banker said. 'I'd be delighted.'

Which should take care of Frank Chaffee. It still left one man for Roth to see—this Judge Henry Gore, who together with Chaffee wielded the balance of political power on the county commission. No love was lost between the Judge and old Sam Hazen—so Roth understood, at least—and this offered interesting possibilities. Moreover, between them Gore and Chaffee controlled the sheriff's office—the final nail needed to pin down Cliff Johnson.

That was how these things worked: Make sure of your key men, and everything else just dropped into place.

An ugly, rawboned horse stood at a tie bar in front of the hotel. It rolled its eyes and laid its ears back and as the two men came past it circled and a hind hoof lashed at Frank

29

Chaffee, missing him by inches. The banker stumbled against Roth and almost fell. 'Vicious brute!' he exploded, glaring at the horse. Roth steadied him, smiling a little. But Chaffee kept on fuming as they went up the steps, crossed the veranda and entered the hotel bar.

The one other customer at the hardwood counter was a man in his fifties, a lank figure in faded denims and jackboots and a shapeless, sweat-stained hat, whose untrimmed black mustache showed streaks of gray. He regarded the newcomers with mildly amused brown eyes—an expression that seemed to infuriate the already angry banker.

'McCune,' Chaffee said hoarsely, settling his rimless glasses, 'did you see what that beast of yours nearly did to me? He could have broken my leg!'

'Reckon I've misjudged you, Frank,' the man said, grinning under the brush of grizzled mustache. 'You're really some spryer than I'd of given you credit for.'

To Roth's observant eye, it was plain the banker didn't relish this use of his first name by a man who had the look of a ne'er-do-well, gone-to-seed nester. Chaffee shrugged irritably, settling his coat on his shoulders. 'You ought to be careful where you tie that animal!'

'Maybe it's other people ought to be careful,' McCune suggested blandly. 'Street belongs to anybody. A man with an eye for horses should know well enough to stay out of his reach.'

Chaffee gave an angry snort and turned his back on the man. He gave the bar-tender his order, in poor grace, and Roth laid money on the bar to pay for both drinks.

'If there's anything I can do,' the banker suggested, 'to help you settle your business here, feel free to call on me.'

Croyden Roth nodded, taking his drink slowly and judiciously. 'That's kind of you,' he said. 'I rode out to have a talk with Sam Hazen yesterday. That Anchor ranch of his interests me, and I'd been given to understand he might be persuaded to make a deal. But—'

He stopped abruptly, scowling in the direction of the scarecrow figure at the other end of the bar. McCune was all too obviously listening, with an idler's interest in other people's affairs. Chaffee set down his glass with a little thump. 'Some men's ears are too big for things that don't concern them,' he remarked, pointedly. 'Let's find a better place to talk.'

They walked out onto the veranda, leaving McCune grinning to himself. Roth produced a couple of his fine cigars and they paused at the top of the porch steps to light up.

'So Sam wouldn't deal?' Frank Chaffee said, reverting to Roth's unfinished statement. 'I could have told you as much. He was one of the first to run beef on this range. I think he intends to be buried on Anchor eventually. I can't see him ever consenting to sell.'

'Sentiment!' Roth murmured, in a tone both mildly scornful and amused. 'At his age, he'd be better off to drop the responsibility and try some part of the country with a milder climate. But every man to his liking.' He took the cigar from his lips, to see how evenly it was burning. Eyes on the smoking tip, he asked casually, 'Mr. Chaffee, what's the Dumont Lease?'

The question drew him the banker's shrewd glance. 'Why, that's a section of land up in the lower hills, between Jack Butte and Medicine Ridge. Good meadow land. Squaw Creek waters it, and there are springs that never seem to fail. A man named Jake Dumont homesteaded the place, years ago.' He watched Roth as he gave this information.

'It's a part of Anchor now?'

'Sam Hazen just has the use of it, on three-year lease. It gives him some of the best grass in the region, and opens directly into the summer range higher up.'

Roth said, 'I suppose your bank holds the patent?'

'No, a private party. The local merchant—a man named William Marshall—bought the land from Jake Dumont years ago and leased it to Hazen. Marshall died this winter. His widow is managing the estate.'

'I see.' Croyden Roth replaced the cigar in

his mouth, rolling it thoughtfully between full, firm lips. Curiosity was plain in the banker's face but Roth had learned what he wanted to know, and confirmed his earlier impressions. He needed to ask no more questions.

*   *   *

Milt McCune, having left the bar by a side entrance, went along the sunbright street at his characteristic long-legged amble. His faded eyes, which usually were deceptively vacant, had been polished to a high gleam of interest by certain things he had just overheard, but an observer passing him on the sidewalk probably would not have noticed. Because his homestead quarter section, on a tributary of the Rock, was a shoddy failure—and because he rode a worthless, crossgrained nag—people were apt to underrate McCune, discounting a native shrewdness he expended on more important matters than mere earning of a living.

True, McCune had followed the gleam of a paying farm for most of his fifty-odd years, across several states and territories. But he considered farming itself to be a nuisance, just an unending series of chores, and in the years since his daughter's marriage to Rock River's leading merchant, Milt McCune had all but given up the pretense of earning the little that he needed.

Coming to the big store building, McCune found his two-year-old grandson playing in the dirt in front of the door. Billy Marshall had been named after his father, but he had the unmistakable black hair and brown eyes of the McCunes. He shouted with delight as Milt grabbed and swung him up, to his favorite perch astride wide, strong shoulders, and they went inside that way, Milt's jackboots thumping echoes from the slab flooring.

A sound of tugging and hauling came from beyond a door at the rear. Milt walked back there, past the counters and storage bins and the racks of harness and tools. He found his daughter Gwen cleaning out a musty storeroom—a hard and dirty job. She had tied a cloth about her head, and without the softening effect of her dark hair she looked drawn and tired and severe. It occurred to McCune that since her husband's death she'd been working much too long and too hard, trying to keep the store going and at the same time do for the little boy.

'Let me,' McCune said gruffly, and setting the youngster down he moved in to take the heavy box Gwen had been trying to lift to a new place on a shelf. He got it up there and stepped back, shaking his head. 'You ought to hire somebody for a job like this.'

'Can't afford it,' she said, in a tone that startled him.

'What do you mean, you can't afford it?'

34

She smiled a little, softening the tired lines of her face; but she still looked tired. 'You can't believe that, can you?' she said. 'Bill Marshall owned a store and you owed him money. So that made him a wealthy man.'

He stiffened and his brows dragged down. 'Now, wait a minute!'

'I know, Dad.' Gwen laid a hand on her father's denimed sleeve. 'You weren't the only one, by any means. The whole range was into him, to some extent—and half the accounts on the books will never be collected. Bill was just that kind, too generous and trusting for his own good.'

Milt McCune ran a palm across his drooping bush of a mustache. 'Why, by gonnies, *I'd* of paid!' he cried indignantly. 'If I'd knowed he needed it, I'd made special effort. But, he never said nothing. Always seemed glad to put it off when I asked for more time. And money ain't been easy to come by. At my time of life, it's tough to make anything out of a quarter section.'

Her brown eyes were searching him again. They didn't seem accusing, exactly, and yet he could feel the warmth of guilt begin to creep upward through his throat, across his stubbled cheeks. Once again he read his own shortcomings in her level scrutiny, seeing himself reflected there as the failure he secretly knew he was—the man who had ever lacked the iron to make a go of any persistent effort.

'Well, anyway,' he said, defensively, 'it was all in the family, wasn't it?'

'Yes, Dad. It was all in the family.'

He almost missed it—and then he caught the undertone in her quiet voice. It struck him like a thunderbolt and made him turn on her with horror clogging his throat.

'Gwen!' His hands reached toward her, fell back trembling. 'I never have figured why you'd go and marry a man twenty years older'n you, when you could of had your pick of any of them! Like that Kindred boy, out at Anchor. Now, there was a man I thought—' Her eyes warned him. Milt stopped, swallowed. But you chose Bill Marshall,' he went on doggedly. 'Could it have been because—'

'Because he bought me? Because he was able to set my father up on a place of his own that we all knew would never pay itself out? Is that what you think?' Gwen's lips tightened until small white lines bracketed them. 'I suppose it must have looked that way to some people. But I assure you, it wasn't!'

'I hope to Gawd it wasn't!' the old man stammered. 'Why, I couldn't stand to think you married him on my account! I ain't never been worth much,' he added, his voice bitter. 'A no-good mover, draggin' my family to hell an' gone around the country until finally your Maw died under it. I sure wasn't worth—'

He broke off, following the direction of her

36

glance toward the little boy. But his grandson, blissfully unaware in the private world of a two-year-old, sat on the floor playing some mysterious game with an empty box.

'Now, get this straight, Dad,' Gwen said, her pretty face sober and intent. 'I married Bill because I wanted to. In three years together he never gave me any cause to regret it. I bore his son. Now Bill's dead, and I'm his widow. It's as simple as that.'

'And what are you going to do now?' he demanded. 'Look at you! You're goin' gaunt, tryin' to run this store. Just what kind of financial hole did he leave you in, anyway?'

She made a tired, formless gesture. 'There's a note at the bank—a big one. I'll get it paid somehow.'

'You'll kill yourself,' McCune growled. Suddenly he laid a hand on his daughter's arm. 'Look! Why not just let the whole thing go to blazes? Drop it before it's too late, and bring the boy and come with me.'

'To that worthless quarter section?' Her mouth firmed; she shook her head. 'No, thanks, Dad. I want something better for Billy than that.'

'Better! Why, what's better than land? Things growin' in the ground—instead of cold metal and paper pilin' up in some damn bank vault—'

'I've heard that all my life,' she reminded him drily. 'And it's never meant anything but

37

unhappiness. I tell you, Billy's going to have the chance to make his life what he wants it. I owe that to him, and to the memory of his father.'

There was no answer for that, and Milt McCune knew it. He took his hand from Gwen's arm and stood mute and unhappy in the musty stillness of the storeroom. The child, playing at their feet, let go a chortle of laughter over some secret joke of his own. Milt looked at the boy, and then the toes of his own scuffed jackboots.

'I been thinkin' some of this fellow Kindred,' he said slowly. 'Have you seen him lately? He's done right well, out there at Anchor. It just occurred to me—'

It was Gwen's turn to go red, and Milt McCune caught the swift rosy blush that made her look like a little girl. She's beautiful, he thought. Even if she is my girl, there ain't more'n a couple other women hereabouts can hold a candle to her. Marriage, and widowhood, had lent her maturity and poise; yet even now she was only twenty-seven.

'You thought,' Gwen said angrily, 'after turning him down for Bill Marshall I could ask Kindred to—to take the responsibility of Bill's child? What do you take me for? Do you suppose I've got no more pride than that?'

Milt frowned. 'I'm not talkin' about pride,' he said bluntly. 'After all, if he was to—'

'But he wouldn't!' Gwen retorted. 'Never in

38

a million years, after what I did to him! It's out of the question!'

Agitation lifted her round, full breast. Her hands were knotted at her sides. Milt, seeing the effect of his casual words, gnawed at the inside of his lower lip. 'How about yourself?' he asked her finally. 'Do you ever think you made a mistake? That you might have liked that fellow a sight more than you knew, but because he was just a ranch foreman and you thought Bill—'

'No!' she cried. 'It isn't true! I—I won't even discuss it!'

'All right,' her father said quickly. He started to leave, and then he snapped his fingers and halted. 'Nearly forgot what I come over to tell you, by God. I think you may be gettin' an offer on that Dumont section.'

She looked blank, uncomprehending. 'What do you mean?'

'There's a stranger in town lookin' for grazin' land—fella named Roth. I happened to hear him asking Frank Chaffee questions. He sounded interested. My guess is you might be hearin' from him.'

'But that property has been under lease to Sam Hazen for years.'

'On whose terms?' he countered shortly. 'Knowin' Bill Marshall, I'll bet Sam's practically had the grass for nothin'. Why don't you look up the contract? Must be about due for renewal. Needin' money as bad as you're goin' to, if you try to keep this store—well, you could do worse than to find out just what this stranger might have in mind, before you sign with Anchor again.'

Gwen Marshall considered this suggestion, frowning. 'Sam Hazen will be counting on using it. It seems hardly fair—'

'Now you're thinkin' like your husband,' McCune said, 'instead of a business woman—which is what you're settin' yourself up to be. It's your problem, girl, but there's one thing to consider. Frank Chaffee and this man Roth look to be on pretty close terms. Chaffee'd probably like real well to see you give Roth a deal if he's interested. You know, with the bank holdin' your note and all. You just might think of that angle.'

Gwen bit her lip and frowned worriedly. McCune grunted in weary resignation.

'That's what goes with ownin' property,' he said with a touch of bitterness. 'Maybe it's one reason I'd just as soon be a failure.'

He started to go again. She did not stop him.

CHAPTER THREE

Unstable as the season itself, the weather changed and shifted. Overnight—within an hour—the pale blue skies of spring gave way to a gray cloud ceiling, and icy rain and swift, slashing sleet. But in another hour it could change again, and once launched on the busy activities of spring roundup the men of that range pushed ahead with it, unmindful of physical discomforts. They carried their slickers on their saddles, and pushed themselves too hard to mind wet clothes and a knifing wind. Range work itself was pleasant, after a monotonous winter of bunkhouse and line camp and stack feeding.

Ed Farrar and young Grady were working together, some distance from the wagon, in a chopped-up stretch of foothill and ravine where cattle had taken refuge in the brush and bad to be pulled out one by one. Riding around to check on their progress, Branch Kindred found them hunkered over a blaze they had been using as a branding fire. A blackened pot of coffee was coming to a boil on the fire, which was protected by the funneling sides of a narrow coulee. Farther back in the brushy cut, some thirty or forty head of cattle that they'd already snaked out milled behind a temporary barrier of ropes and brush. Their melancholy bellowing mingled with the organ-tone of a cold, wet wind that combed the rocky breaks. Scraps of snow still lay about on the dark wet ground. Mist rose from the flanks and nostrils of the horses.

The two hands grinned as their boss rode

up. 'Light,' Ed Farrar invited. 'This stuff'll be hot enough in a minute, so you can maybe feel it going down.'

'Thanks,' Kindred said, and dismounted, putting his horse with the others. He joined the men at the fire, squatting to warm his hands at the blaze. The cramped walls of the coulee helped deflect the wind here, but cross-drafts caught the smoke and swirled it into their faces. Scattered near the fire was a pile of branding irons—the Anchor brand, and a couple of running irons for putting the proper mark on any stray calf from some neighbor's cow that might have got in here.

'How's it going?' Farrar wanted to know.

'Good enough. No winter kill to speak of—and that was a tough one. Another day and we'll have enough to begin shoving them up onto the Lease.'

Gray jerked his head toward the penned beef behind them. 'We've about cleaned up this section. We might need some help bringing what we've got down to the day herd. They're pretty ringy. They'll head back for the timber, given half a chance.'

'I'll stick around and give you a hand,' Kindred said.

The pot came to a boil and Farrar snaked it from the coals with a rope-tough hand that didn't mind the heat of the metal handle. Lacking cups, they passed the pot around, taking turns drinking directly from the spout

42

and straining the grounds through their teeth.

'Any word from the girl?' Ed Farrar asked Kindred.

'Judy? Should be in tomorrow, I think. I'm meeting the stage.'

'To prepare her for the shock, I suppose?' Tom Grady suggested, and made a sour face. 'I wonder what the hell she's gonna think of her paw when she finally meets him!'

'What I'd like to know,' Farrar said, 'is how a thing like him ever got himself wedged into the same family tree between two such people as Sam and Judy Hazen. He don't belong. It just don't figure.'

Kindred understood their thinking but as foreman he could not allow indiscriminate gossip about the Hazens. 'It isn't any of our business,' he reminded them shortly. 'We won't worry about it.'

Ed Farrar scowled and swirled the coffee pot, judging how much was left of its contents. 'Sam's worried,' he said. 'I can tell. I don't like the way he's been acting since that son of his got home. Hardly even stirs out of that rockin' chair in the front room. And his color—' He shook his head. 'I don't like it!' he repeated.

Branch had said nothing to the men about Sam's condition, judging it none of their concern. Now he wondered if this had been wise. Maybe he ought to take an old hand like Ed Farrar into his confidence. But still he bided his time.

'It's enough to put any man off his feed,' Tom Grady said darkly, 'having that Earl Hazen dropped into his lap. What's the matter with the man, anyhow? I never seen such a surly, no-account bastard. You'd think the crew was dirt under his boots or something. Seems to me—'

'Watch it!' Kindred warned sharply.

The others saw his glance go past them, and heard the horsemen at the same instant. They swiveled about, and at sight of the two riders bearing toward them Ed Farrar gave a grunt and set the coffee pot back into the coals. 'Speak of the devil,' he muttered. 'And who is it Hazen's got with him? Why, it's that Roth gent.'

Very quietly Kindred eased to his feet. He had not yet met the stranger, and curiosity beat high in him as he waited for the first encounter.

The moan of the wind had covered sound of the riders until they had nearly reached the fire. It was not raining at the moment, but they both wore yellow slickers that gave them a bulky look. Earl Hazen's horse was an Anchor mount. Roth's sorrel had come from the livery in town, and while it was a good-sized animal, Kindred judged that the man it carried was no lightweight. Roth filled the saddle solidly, his boots deep in the stirrups. He seemed as much at home there as Earl Hazen appeared ill at ease.

The newcomers pulled rein beside the fire. Earl Hazen looked around—at the fire, the horses, the branding irons. 'What happens here?' he demanded, in his sour tone.

'Collecting a few bad ones out of the brush,' Ed Farrar told him; he indicated the crude corral that had been formed by fencing off the throat of the coulee above them. 'We always have to work over this stretch a second time, to get them all.'

Hazen gave a grumpy nod. In this wind, apparently, he'd missed the stir and bellow of cattle behind the fence, and even now he evinced no real interest in them. Ranch work seemed to mean nothing to him. Blue-lipped and irritable, he showed in his very posture that he didn't like the saddle, didn't like the damp cold, and didn't like the rough country he'd bumped and jounced through to get here.

Croyden Roth's attention had been drawn to Kindred as to a magnet, from the moment he pulled rein. The two men studied one another with a wary interest, Branch Kindred sensing that Roth had guess who he was. For his own part, he found something about the big man's smooth rather heavy features that repelled him.

Plainly, he thought, this was a tour of inspection. Roth was sizing up the ranch he meant to buy.

Earl Hazen saw them sizing each other up.

45

To Roth he said gruffly, 'This is the man I told you about.'

'The foreman,' Roth said, and nodded. 'I've been waiting to meet you,' he told the man beside the fire. 'It's Kindred, isn't it? My name is Roth.'

Kindred shoved his thumbs behind the buckle of his belt. He stood with muddy boots spread a little apart, and he made no move to offer his hand. Roth started to shift his weight in the saddle, then straightened, brought his own hand back and laid it on the horn. A frown bunched his cheek muscles briefly, ironed itself out and left his face expressionless.

'From New Mexico,' Branch Kindred said. 'What part of New Mexico would that be?'

'I have quite a few interests down there, in various sections,' the big man said. As though unaware that he had failed to answer the question, he added, 'Right now, I'm looking this range over. A good property the Hazens have there—'

'Earl,' Kindred said, 'maybe you forgot to tell Mr. Roth that Anchor isn't for sale?'

Hazen scowled but Roth passed the remark off. 'Maybe the right price just hasn't been offered.'

'Anchor hasn't got a price!'

'Oh, come now,' Roth said, and his broad mouth quirked a little at the ends. 'Everything does—you know that. My business is finding

46

out just what the right price is.

'Well, my business at present,' Kindred said, working to hold rein on his temper, 'is getting Anchor beef counted and started for summer range. I better be at it.'

He stepped over to his horse. He had had enough of talking to this pair and he saw no point in continuing it. He heard Ed Farrar growl, 'Yeah. Come along, Grady. You and me got a couple more pockets to clean out.'

The two Anchor riders climbed into saddle, but Kindred had first to yank the cinch tight on his roan. Farrar and Grady were already jogging away into the drifting mists before Kindred smoothed down the stirrup leather and reached to gather the reins.

'Mr. Kindred,' Roth said, behind him, and he turned. The big man had leaned forward, a forearm resting on the pommel. The swollen, wind-pushed clouds were letting down rain now, a slow drizzle that stung a man's face and hands and made small sizzling noises in the fire. Kindred waited, rein in hand, looking up at the mounted men.

'There's something I have in mind to say which I think might be of interest to you,' Croyden Roth told him. 'You see, if I do make a satisfactory deal for this property I'm going to be in the market for a manager—a good one, who not only knows cattle but understands the particular problems of this particular range. I'll pay top salary to the right man. It would seem rather obvious that you're likely the one I need, Kindred.'

For a long moment Kindred just sat there, numb with disbelief. Then a hard knot of anger formed in his chest, constricting his breathing. He felt the nails dig into his palms as his hands clenched, and he said tightly, 'You've made a mistake. I'm not for sale any more than Anchor is, Mr. Roth.'

Their stares locked, in a complete mutual understanding. There was not the slightest chance that either had misinterpreted the other. *Don't stand in my way,* Roth had said, in effect. *Help convince old Hazen to sell, at my figure, and as a reward I'll up whatever salary he pays you.* And the rock-hard defiance of Kindred's refusal was no less plain.

Roth's eyes changed, subtly, then— hardened with anger that contained threat and a warning. With a grunt and a grimace that pulled his mouth into an ugly shape, he straightened in saddle and took up the reins. A booted heel kicked the rent horse and it sprang forward under him.

More slowly, Earl Hazen spoke to his own horse and followed. The two figures in their yellow slickers rode away into the drizzling rain. Kindred stood with fury boiling in him, and watched them out of sight.

* * *

Breath made a mist in front of Earl Hazen's face as he caught up to Croyden Roth. He shivered, teeth chattering, and cursed the icy rain and the clammy folds of the slicker. 'This damn country!' he muttered, hunching shoulders. 'How can anybody stand it?'

'Be glad you're not on roundup,' Roth told him.

'And some people wonder why I got out of here when I did!' Hazen went on fuming. 'What would my life have been good for if I'd stayed? I'd been no better off than any of these stupid cowhands—going through the same miserable routine, summer and winter, year after year, until the country broke me the way it's broken my father! What kind of existence is that?'

'A matter of temperament,' Roth said. 'Your man Kindred would never agree.'

'Kindred's a fool!'

'I'm not so sure,' Roth murmured, as if thinking aloud.

'Your point of view, now, I can understand,' Hazen plunged on, shoving a hand into his pocket to warm it. 'It's a business proposition with you. To buy a ranch and hire some character to do the riding and buck the weather, and send the proceeds to you in Denver or Frisco: That makes sense,' he said enviously. 'But it takes a knack I haven't got. I don't fool myself—not any more. I'll never be a rich man.'

Suddenly the rain became a downpour that slapped into the earth and surrounded them with blowing silver curtains. It happened so fast that the horses came to an uneasy stand, nervously tossing their heads. Earl Hazen swore fiercely.

Roth was fastening his slicker. 'We'd better be getting down,' he said, speaking loudly above the smash of the rain. 'We'll see nothing more in this sort of thing, and it could keep it up the rest of the day.'

'Come on with me, to the house. We can dry out there, and find something to drink.'

'No.' Water runneled from Roth's hatbrim as he shook his head. 'I'm for town. Thanks anyway—also, for showing me around. I've learned what I need. I've got an idea of the ranch, now. After I've done some figuring, I'll be riding out to make the old man an offer and see if we can't arrange a deal.'

'You'll be wise to do it when that man Kindred isn't around,' Earl Hazen suggested darkly. 'I have an idea he's going to prove the big stumbling block. Dad holds out, I think, mostly because he has him to lean on.'

Roth said nothing to that. He rode on into the rain in a moody silence, scarcely noticing when his trail and Hazen's parted. But suddenly, alone, he pulled up and twisted to look behind him. An idea had taken form all in an instant. Roughly, he pulled his rent horse around again.

50

The animal balked, not wanting to turn back into the full force of the rain and the wind blowing down from the higher hills, but Roth used a firm hand and a ready spur. Pine trees whipped and swayed above him, brush creaked before the gusty wind. With an outdoorsman's sure instinct, Roth took only a few minutes retracing his course. As he rode he climbed, and so came at last into the comparative quiet of a fringe of timber that edged the rim of the coulee where he'd met Branch Kindred.

There he halted, rising in the stirrups for a careful look.

Behind the brush fence, the imprisoned cattle were a stirring of wet hides in the rain, and their protesting mutter rose to him. He saw Branch Kindred ride into the coulee, swinging a rope and choosing a couple of steers ahead of him. The foreman's shouts reached Roth as he drove the animals up to the gate. It was a tricky job for one man to get the gate open and push the steers through it; but they went without too much persuading, once they heard the bellowing of those others already in the pen. Kindred closed the barrier and turned back.

The fire had been nearly knocked out by the rain and was smouldering fitfully, sending off heavy clouds of smoke. Roth watched Kindred dismount and walk over to throw more wood on it, trying to keep it alive. The rain had eased again but the wind was as wild as ever.

Kindred stood beside the blaze, a foreshortened figure in a black rubber poncho. A gun appeared in Croyden Roth's fingers. He lowered it again. He had an easy shot here but it would be a mistake to take it—entirely too obvious. Then a better alternative occurred to him. He mulled it over and reached his decision. He reined away, holstering the gun and already beginning to work at the fastening of his slicker.

He had it off by the time he reached the head of the coulee. There was a fairly steep dropoff. The rent horse tried to rear and turn back; Roth jabbed the steel and the sorrel took the descent to the coulee floor, slipping and nearly falling on slick rock surfaces. Then they had reached the level with the cattle stirring around them.

The slicker in Roth's hand rose, circling. He brought it down against a bony rump. A steer blatted in terror and lunged against its neighbors. He swung again, laying about him with the crackling rubber garment. Already upset by the storm, and by the treatment they'd taken at the hands of the Anchor riders, these half-wild animals swerved and scattered ahead of him.

Roth crowded them hard. The flapping slicker struck and whirled and struck again. Terror filled the bawling of the steers as they lunged wildly away, and was transmitted through the steers jammed up together in that narrow-walled cut. The whole bunch lumbered into a run.

Driving ahead, risking the murderous horns, Roth heard a splintering crash as they hit the flimsy brush-and-rope barrier and went smashing through. At once, he pulled rein, so sharply that the trembling sorrel sagged back on its haunches. When it tried to rear he cursed it down.

*   *   *

The wind pushed hard against Kindred as he stood waiting for Grady and Farrar to come in with the last of the steers, so that they could get this bunch started down to open country and the day herd. It whipped the bulky folds of the poncho, howled along the rims of the coulee, carried away from his ears any warning of commotion in the pen twenty yards behind him. When the barrier went crashing down he whirled, startled, to see frightened steers lunging straight toward him through the narrow funnel.

He was pawing the wet rubber, trying to get at his gun, even as he realized it would do no good. Bullets wouldn't stop them. They would be on him before he could get off more than a single shot or two across their frenzied, lowered heads.

Forgetting the gun, he turned to look for his horse. He saw the roan aheady plunging away,

53

ears laid back, too frightened to heed the dangling reins.

The ground trembled to the rush of stampeding hoofs. For what seemed like a frozen, suspended moment in time, he stood watching a rushing wall of horns and rolling eyeballs and plummeting hoofs. Then he was running—awkwardly, on high-heeled boots— toward the nearer wall of the cut.

He knew it was going to be close, so close that he couldn't guess at his chances of making it. From the tail of his eye he saw the lunging bulk of a steer and the gleam of a horn, and tried to twist aside. A strong-muscled shoulder slammed into him and flung him bodily forward and down. He stabbed both palms flat against the muddy ground and caught himself, pushed to his feet again. As he stumbled ahead he felt a horn tip catch the rubber poncho and rip it to the hem before tearing free. Thrown off balance, he staggered and then, at last, gained the coulee's bank.

He threw himself against it, whirling to press his shoulders flat against the rock. Panting, he watched the wild cattle pound past him. One steer, shoved against him, struck his leg with a crippling weight. Then as quickly as it started, the stampede ended and the cattle were free of the coulee and scattering into the brush and timber.

Kindred peered blearily at the wreckage of the brush fence, at the hoof-trampled mud and the smoldering wreckage of what had been a fire until that juggernaut rolled over it. His mind cleared and his first thought was: *How could a man be so stupid as to let himself get caught in a thing like that?* But even as he condemned himself, he knew that wasn't the real question. The brush barrier, flimsy as it was, should have been strong enough to hold those steers under any expected circumstance.

Something had spooked them. A cougar? Maybe.

A few minutes later he heard a shout, and Ed Farrar came spurring into the mouth of the coulee. Farrar had caught up Kindred's roan. He was leading it on trailing reins, and his face looked white and sick under the pushed-back, rain-drenched sodbuster. He pulled up and stared at his boss.

'What in God's name?' he said huskily. 'I seen them beefs scooting to hell an' gone and your bronc running crazy in the midst of them. I thought something had happened to you, for sure.'

'They broke out,' Kindred said. He limped a little as he walked over to his horse and swung into the saddle. The roan was still scared and he had to speak to it to settle it.

'Let's take a look around, Ed.'

Farrar just grunted when he saw the wreckage of the gate. He followed Kindred, matching his foreman's slow pace riding up into the narrow throat of the coulee. Kindred

55

kept examining the ground yard by yard and finally the puncher asked, 'Maybe I could help if I knew what you were looking for.'

'I'm not sure myself,' Kindred said, and in the next breath he tightened the rein with a suddenness that made the uneasy roan toss its head and mouth the bit. 'This, maybe,' he said, and pointed.

Farrar, riding up even with him, saw it: the print of an iron shoe, in a patch of mud. 'Big as a frypan,' he said. 'That wasn't one of our horses. And anyhow, we didn't none of us ride in this far.'

'But someone did,' Kindred said. 'I think he must have dropped down into the head of this coulee, from the bank.'

'And spooked them steers?' Farrar said, and then sucked in his breath as if he'd startled himself. 'You think he maybe deliberately tried to run them over you?'

Kindred didn't answer, but a bleak certainty had taken hold of him. Farrar looked at the hooftrack again. 'Roth was forking an outsize bronc,' he said slowly. 'That big sorrel from the livery in Rock River. Yeah! It would have made a print this size. But—what are you going to do about it, Chief?'

'Right now,' Kindred said, 'we'll keep quiet. We don't know anything for sure. Let's not go jumping at conclusions in public.'

'You going to let him have another chance to kill you, then?'

'Not if I can help it. But whatever we suspect, there's reasons we have to keep this to ourselves. One, it will help to let Roth think we don't know anything, so we can watch to see how far he's really willing to go. For another—'

'I guess I know,' Farrar cut in. 'Earl Hazen. We don't know whether he had any part in this, or knew about it.'

Kindred nodded soberly. 'For old Sam's sake,' he said, 'and Judy's—we have to be damned sure.'

*   *   *

Croyden Roth was in a poor mood by the time be reached the hotel—chilled, rain-soaked, and deeply chagrined over his failure to catch Branch Kindred in that stampede. He had delayed no longer than to make sure that the foreman had escaped. If Kindred should get the notion that the spooking of that herd had been no accident, it wouldn't pay for him to be found in the vicinity.

With his rented sorrel checked in at the livery barn, Roth tramped the block to his hotel room and a change of clothes. The rain had thinned out and stopped, but a cold wind ruffled the puddles in the street and knifed through his soggy garments, adding nothing to his mood. Roth was a man who kept a stern control of himself, but he did not like to be crossed. Now that he had taken a look for

57

himself at the lie of this range, the advantage in gaining control of Sam Hazen's ranch seemed more desirable than ever. Earl Hazen was a fool who would give no trouble. His father was sick and old, and lacking a prop should be easy enough to get around eventually. But that prop still stood.

At the lobby desk, getting his key, he mumbled in answer to the clerk's obsequious comments on the weather. Behind him, near the murky window, a newspaper rustled. Turning toward the stairs, Roth glanced over there and halted in midstride as he saw a man rise from one of the sagging leather chairs.

'This gentleman was asking for you, Mr. Roth,' the clerk said. He went unanswered. Jay Benteen folded his newspaper and shoved it into a coat pocket as he crossed the faded carpet toward Roth. He was a rangy man, a scowling man just now. His hard-thrust jaw bore a stubble of whiskers that glinted faintly red; his thick mop of wiry hair was red, as well. His nose had been broken in some saloon or trail camp in the past and it lay crookedly against his face. He said, 'I been settin' in this chair for a couple of hours.'

'Come up to the room,' Roth told him, and led the way. The staircase swayed and groaned under their solid tramping.

With the door closed and locked again behind them, they stood facing each other in this dingy room whose only furnishings

58

consisted of a swaybacked bed, a straight chair, and a soap-spattered washstand. Knowing the thinness of the wall, Roth kept his voice down. 'Well!' he said as he tossed his hat and slicker onto the chair. 'I guess you got my wire from Kansas City. You made damn good time—I wasn't expecting you for another week. You must have run the legs off that herd.'

Benteen shook his bullet head. 'The herd's three days down the trail. I left Hooker in charge and come ahead as fast as I could ride. I had to get you the news.'

'What news?' Roth knew it was going to be bad—probably disastrous, to judge from Benteen's manner and his haste to bring it. But he managed to appear quite cold and calm as he waited.

His trail boss fetched up the newspaper he had brought with him. It was not a local paper; Rock River had none. This was a Gunnison weekly, and Benteen had folded it back to a story on an inner page.

'I'll let *you* read it,' he said, and handed it over.

It was only a paragraph, with a New Mexico dateline. Quickly skimming, Croyden Roth read about a local official whose confession of accepting bribes from a land and cattle company had called for a sudden and thorough investigation of the company's operations, the impounding of its bank funds and facilities, and a search as to the

59

whereabouts of an important official. He read it again as he fought to collect his thoughts. He had seen this coming, but not so soon!

Jay Benteen flopped onto the bed, the springs skrealing under him. 'It was that bastard Ferguson did the talking,' he said. 'The pressure finally got too strong and he broke wide open. Way it happened, there wasn't a chance to salvage anything except that thousand head we had ready for the trail. I pushed it right along—couldn't risk having the sheriff's office catch up with us and put an attachment on the herd or something.'

'You were right. How many of the men did you bring away with you?'

'Twenty. Practically the whole bunch. I knew that whatever you did, you'd be wanting them.' Benteen indicated the newspaper. 'I picked that up a couple days back. Looks like the news didn't take long to spread this far.'

Roth gnawed at his lip. There was one all-important point that he hadn't failed to notice in this briefly-worded account: By a lucky fluke, it carried no mention of his own name, only that of the company behind which he'd operated. And there was, he felt sure, no immediate way that anyone here in Colorado would be apt to link the two together. With luck, they never would.

Considering this one stroke of good fortune, he tossed the paper aside and walked to the

60

window, to stand frowning thoughtfully through rain-spotted glass into the street below. Already he was working at the edges of the disaster—the worst that had ever befallen him—for he was a practical man who wasted no time on pointless brooding.

Coldly, he weighed the situation. No doubt the authorities had already dug up enough facts about his operations in New Mexico to make it impossible for him ever to set foot there again. That left him a thousand head of cattle, trail-hungry and needing grass which he didn't own to put them on; a few hundred dollars in his wallet and a twenty-man crew to be paid; a bank draft in his pocket which had suddenly turned into a worthless piece of paper. Little enough, but he'd been in worse spots.

'So what are you going to do?' Benteen said.

Well, first there would be the problem of finding range for the cattle Benteen had managed to salvage. Buying Anchor was out of the question now. He might be able to work something on Earl Hazen and that banker, but neither old Sam nor Branch Kindred was apt to be taken in. The bank draft would obviously be of no use. He couldn't have anyone on this range making enquiries which would turn up the damaging facts about his New Mexico operations. He had nothing to work with but the money in his pocket.

He turned from the window, gave his trail

boss a lax smile. 'Do?' he repeated, and shrugged indifferently. 'Don't worry. I'll think of something.'

CHAPTER FOUR

Branch Kindred was working on a close budget of time these days, with not hours enough to accomplish all the things he needed to. It was already past stage time when he rode his dusty, stockinged roan into the main street at Rock River. He could have told off one of the crew to come in, but he felt that he should make the trip himself. Certain things ought to be said to augment the rather skimpy wordage of the telegram to Montrose, and prepare Judy Hazen for what she would find when she got home. He didn't want to leave this to anyone else.

The coach hadn't yet arrived, apparently. He saw the usual crowd of kids and loafers still gathered in front of the station at the foot of the long street, and he let some of the pressure lift from him as his cowpony carried him along the rutted street at a swinging trot. It was a good, crisp day, under a warm spring sky that was dappled with clouds—the aftermath of the breakup of recent rains. The cottonwoods that eased the bleak pattern of this town's raw buildings were shaking their new leaves in the sun.

A woman came out of the bank, leading a little boy by the hand. Her head was bent toward the child but Kindred would have known her anywhere—the slim-waisted figure, the glossy blackness of her hair with its center part like a ruled white line. Even now, after the passage of three years during which she had belonged to another man, Gwen Marshall could cause an unsettled churning somewhere in his middle. He felt his mouth go dry. His eyes would not quit her, and it might have been the very weight of his stare that made Gwen look up and then straighten as he rode abreast of where she stood.

Kindred drew in the rein, nearly halting the bronc. He touched his hat brim and nodded a greeting, watching her lips and her dark eyes. He had exchanged no word with her since her husband's death, but at any sign that she wanted to speak to him now he would have pulled up and stepped down beside her. She did return the nod, a very faint gesture. Her lips parted but the invitation went unspoken. And then, in the doorway behind her, Frank Chaffee said something and Gwen turned to answer, and the moment passed.

Kindred smiled at the little boy, who still regarded him with humorless brown eyes that were a replica of his mother's. And then he rode on, again unsmiling, leaving Gwen Marshall and Chaffee to talk business on the steps of the barnlike red building.

Business, he thought, and shrugged. She had married a store when she married the storekeeper, and she must have known what she wanted. He could not begrudge her her choice.

The stage office with its storage sheds and stock corral closed off the north end of the long, crooked street, faced by a wide turnaround which the drivers always used to stop their coaches before the station with a flourish and a sweep of powdered dust. At this time of afternoon, on the days of the run, a scatter of idlers could ordinarily be found roosting along the corral bars and the knife-scarred benches on the porch, whittling and chewing gossip and waiting for the excitement of stage time. When Kindred tied up his roan and walked over to join them, he was not at all surprised to find Milt McCune leaning his lanky shape against a roof-prop with one dusty boot jacked across the other, a knife and a slab of pine in his hands. Milt belonged with this bunch. He nodded to Kindred, slack and lackadaisical but friendly enough.

'Well!' he said. 'Things so slack out at Anchor that you got nothin' to do but join the whittlin' society?'

'I've got plenty to do,' Kindred answered dryly. 'Right now I'm meeting the Montrose stage.'

Milt McCune inspected his handiwork. He

put the wood to pursed lips and blew a fine cloud of yellow shavings. 'A boat,' he explained, as though Kindred had asked. 'Makin' it for Silly. Won't even float, I suppose.' He examined the block of wood critically, from every direction, head craned back and one eye half closed.

'Bringin' the girl home, eh?' he said then, as he went back to his carving. 'Cuttin' that visit kind of short, ain't you? Still, I guess there's reasons.'

Kindred said nothing. As he watched Milt McCune's big hands, which were adept enough with a whittling blade but seemed oddly inexpert at any task of a more profitable nature, it struck him that few men knew more about things that concerned them less. A thoroughly impractical type, McCune, and probably a hard one for any woman to have had to depend on. Yet Kindred had always liked him well enough.

'Judy's gotten to be right pretty, lately,' Milt said.

'You'll get no argument on that score.'

A long sliver of pinewood curled up around the sliding blade, clean and yellow in the sunlight. 'You kind of like her, I guess?'

Kindred studied him closely but could read nothing behind the question. It seemed a strange one, coming from the man who might have been his father-in-law. Kindred took his time answering, and when he did he picked his words carefully and spoke them with a deliberate slowness that made his meaning clear. 'She's a very nice little girl, Milt.'

'Well, yes—she's young. About seventeen, now?'

'Nineteen.'

Milt raised an eyebrow. 'Seems younger. Gwen, now, at her age—' He lifted his gaunted shoulders. 'Still, I guess it's how they grow makes the difference. Judy's had things pretty good—solid rancher for a grandsire, easy livin', whatever she fancied toted to her on a platter. Nothin' like that behind Gwen. Pillar to post, for that lady. Can't rightly say she ever was give much chance to be a little girl, at all. Picked the wrong pa, I guess.' He said it without self condemnation, merely as an observation. He blew wood dust from his carving again and added, 'On the other hand, from what I've seen of him I couldn't exactly say that Judy picked much better!'

Kindred didn't intend to be drawn into this line of discussion. He shoved his hands into his hip pockets and ran a frowning stare along the empty street. He noticed a ball of drying mud stuck to the edge of the porch where someone had scraped his boot during the recent wet weather. Deliberately, he kicked it to dust.

Then a whooping of distant dogs and a growing racket of wheels and hoofs announced the advent of the stagecoach into Rock River. All talk ended along the roofed porch as the

66

big stage came rocking into view at the far end of the long street and careered toward them, a wild rush behind six straining, head-tossing horses. Loose scraps of paper fluttered in the suction of its wheels, and the town dogs bayed hoarsely in a pack behind.

No self-respecting whip ever ended his run with anything but a flourish. The horses hit the turn-around before the station, making the circle in a wide sweep that lifted the heavy coach onto two wheels, and suddenly piling up to a halt with brake shoe screaming. It rocked violently on the leather braces, and through the drift of dust, the scared faces of the passengers could be seen as they clung desperately to anything within reach.

But when Branch Kindred lifted Judy Hazen down the high step, she was laughing and breathless. He set her on her feet and she tried to pat her postage stamp hat into place on bright, wind-wrecked curls, while her blue eyes danced with amused excitement. 'I must look a mess!' she cried.

'You look perfect. Have a nice visit?'

'Oh, just wonderful. The Hislops treated me fine.'

'They better,' Kindred declared, beaming at her. He took her elbow then, drawing her out of the confusion around the coach and up onto the station porch. He found Milt McCune watching them with an expressionless intentness. The older man nodded shortly and

Judy threw him one of her generous smiles and said, 'Hi, Milt.' But she was looking for something, and when she saw Kindred's stockinged roan tied by itself to a hitch-pole she asked quickly, 'But where's Boots?'

'Eating his head off at the ranch,' Kindred said. 'I didn't know if you'd rather ride or have me fetch a rig from the livery.'

'Oh, ride!' She made a face. 'I never want wheels under me again! I'm all over bruises!' She clucked ruefully at herself, smoothed her rumpled traveling dress.

'Hungry?'

'Famished!'

'Well, then, let's go up to the hotel and see if there's anything decent on the menu. Afterward you can change while I'm getting a horse for you.'

That suited her fine. 'I'll need the small handbag, Branch. The leather one. I packed jeans and things in there.'

'All right.' He pestered the harried station agent until he got the article handed out of the boot at the back of the stage, and arranged for the girl's larger suitcase to be held until it could be picked up. Then, taking Judy's warm round arm, he escorted her across the wheel-churned space before the station and on toward the hotel. Milt McCune, unmoving from his lazy stance against the post, idly whittled and watched them go with his expressionless brown gaze.

In the hotel dining room, Kindred sipped at a cup of coffee while Judy made a meal of the indifferent food. She was a hearty eater, with none of the false delicacy about such matters that city girls liked to affect. But a change had come into her manner, after the first excitement of arrival. She seemed grave, now, and finally she asked the question he knew had been gnawing at her.

'Why did you want me home, Branch? The wire didn't say very much.'

'I know.' He lifted his coffee cup, scowled and set it in the heavy china saucer. 'That's the reason I wanted to have this talk, before we started for the ranch. There are a couple of things I have to tell you, Judy. The first is about your grandfather—'

He saw Judy's eyes widen and darken. Her lips parted, formed the word, 'No!'

'Don't be startled,' he said quickly. 'It isn't that. But Sam is ill, Judy, He didn't want you to know this, but you'd have seen it for yourself. I think it's kinder to break the news to you now, instead of let you have a shock when you see him.'

She, touched the tip of her tongue to her upper lip. 'How—how bad is he?'

'It's his heart. You can't trust it too much, when you get to his age, you know. He may get along all right, last for a long time yet. But no one can be sure.' He added gently, 'Seemed to me you were old enough to be told this—and

69

then not to let Sam see that you know.'

'Yes.' Her voice was very faint. She picked up her fork and put it down again. 'Thank you for being honest with me, Branch.' She sat in silence for a moment, and then, when Kindred did not speak, she reminded him, 'You said you had a couple of things to tell me. What's the other one?'

'The other matter is maybe not for me to discuss with you, Judy. But I think you'd have a right to wonder why I didn't say something, anyhow, to prepare you. It's about someone you don't remember. Someone I suppose you never really thought you'd ever see—'

He paused, a little alarmed by the way the color had fled from her face. Judy's hand tightened on the edge of the table and her cheeks were ashen. 'My father! He's here!'

Kindred nodded.

'What—what is he like?'

'No point in my trying to tell you that. You'll be meeting him shortly.'

'I don't want to!' she exclaimed. Her voice sank to an anguished whisper. 'I hate him!'

'You can't mean that, Judy.'

'I do mean it!' Her head lifted, and color tinging her cheeks now. Her young round breast began to rise on breath quickened by emotion. 'Why shouldn't I, after what he did to us? Running away, leaving Gramps stuck with me to look after. And—and leaving—' Her eyes brightened with tears. 'A girl needs a father, Branch! It would have been hard enough if—if he'd been dead. But to know, all these years, that he was alive, somewhere—that he just didn't want me—'

Her mouth began to tremble. The tears spilled over. She turned blindly away and put her hands before her face.

At first Kindred could only sit there, numb with sympathy and at a loss to know what he should do. But then he got to his feet and came around the table and placed a hand on her shoulder. 'Judy—'

Straightening quickly, she managed a wan smile. 'I'm all right. And I do thank you for telling me, Branch. I'll be better able to meet him now.'

He squeezed her shoulder and dropped his hand. 'I'll see about the horses,' he said gruffly. 'Whenever you're ready, we can go.'

*   *   *

Judy came down the creaking stairs from the room where she had gone to change her clothes. She was wearing jeans and a white silk blouse that molded her young figure with an unconscious charm. Instead of the little postage stamp hat, a blue scarf encircled her head with the tied ends dangling between her shoulders. The crisp, curling ends of short hair the color of ripe wheat eased the severity of the head cloth, and her eyes matched the

71

shade of it so that it made them seem enormous. The desk clerk swallowed as Judy dimpled a smile of thanks and laid the key in front of him. Carrying her leather traveling bag, Judy walked out onto the porch and paused at the top of the veranda steps.

Pine scent, like a heady wine, tanged the warm afternoon and she breathed it deeply, filled with the contentment of being home. The first stunned shock of Branch Kindred's news had passed, leaving her a little guilty and ashamed at herself for the way she had taken it. You acted like a baby, she told herself, and wondered what on earth Branch must have thought.

But he had behaved with infinite kindness and understanding, in wanting to prepare her for what she would find, and then in accepting and passing off the manner of her reaction. A warm affection for Branch filled her, as she stood there in the sun and waited for him to bring the horses for the ride home to Anchor.

Two men came out of the bar at the other end of the hotel veranda and approached the steps. Judy drew closer to the prop post to make way for them. The steps were wide and there should have been plenty of room, but the man who jostled her might have had a drink or so too many. He brushed against her heavily. She staggered, dropped the leather bag—and put a hand against the post. As she did she caught the unpleasant mingling of sweat and

72

alcohol. The man mumbled something, and a big hand closed upon her arm near the elbow—either to steady her, or himself.

'Sorry,' he grunted.

He was a stranger. She'd never seen this face with its crooked nose, this close-cropped patch of red hair that furred the top of the bullet head. She gave a little shiver of distaste and tried to shake off the hand. But the hand tightened its grip. Powerful fingers pressed deeper into her soft flesh, and with a tingle of alarm she noticed the shine in his eyes.

'Let go of me, please,' she said.

The man began to grin. 'Hey, now!' he said thickly. 'You wouldn't cold-shoulder me? Ain't you the blonde I was with night before last, in that house on Fremont Street?'

She felt the heat begin to spread through her throat and face, and then fear replaced it as she saw how really drunk he was. Her glance moved wildly past to his companion. Blue eyes in a weak face did not reassure her. The second stranger wet his lips and said, in ineffectual protest, 'Go easy, Benteen. I think you're making a mistake.'

But the redhead paid no attention, and plainly there was no help here. Judy forgot the second man. To this Benteen she said in a voice she couldn't keep from trembling, 'You take your hand off my arm, or you're going to wish you had!'

The grin turned ugly. 'The hell with you,'

Benteen said harshly. 'You was friendly enough the other night!' He lurched against her. His other arm came up, started to slide about her waist. She felt his breath on her face and her throat clogged. She got both hands against his chest, feeling the muscular hardness through the heavy woolen shirt, and pushed him violently away.

The heel of Benteen's boot slid over the edge of the top step and threw him off balance. He went stumbling backward down the steps, arms pinwheeling to save him from a spill. He ended up by swinging sideward into the rail, with a force that nearly split it. Arms spread wide, he leaned there and looked up at Judy's white face.

'Now wait just a minute,' he said softly.

Still the yellow-haired, blue-eyed man did nothing, said nothing, and that section of the street appeared to be deserted. Judy stooped and caught up her traveling bag. She really ought to have run back into the hotel, but her one thought was to get past these men, away from this place and into the open. She started down the steps, cutting toward the opposite railing, trying to swing wide of Benteen.

But he wasn't ready to let her go. He leaped away from the pole at his back and caught her. A choked scream broke from Judy's throat and she swung at him with the ineffectual leather case. She slipped and fell in a sprawl on the steps, nearly pulling Benteen down on top of

74

her.

Then a hand closed on Benteen's shoulder, a hand that jerked him back and tore him loose from the girl and spun him clear around.

'You goddam scum,' Branch Kindred said, and he struck Benteen in the middle of his sweaty face. His other fist came up and landed soggily on the side of the jaw. Benteen sprawled on the hard dirt path in front of the hotel.

For a moment he lay there, on his back, squinting up into the sun while blood made a bright smear on his mouth. And then with a bellow of rage he came bouncing up again, the whisky fog totally knocked out of him. There was a gun at his hip but he seemed to prefer the direct way of physical combat. Judy, stumbling to her feet, cried out in alarm as she saw the man rush Kindred. Then she saw Branch fade back a pace and meet the charge. She heard the thudding slap of fists, and she wanted to run away, and she couldn't. She had to watch this. She *had* to.

Benteen was the heavier man and he drove Kindred back, with a blow to the ribs that flung him against a tie-rail. The pair of horses he'd left there on trailing reins shied a little, with nervous tosses of their heads. Benteen started to close with his man but Kindred, waiting until the last second, ducked away from the pole and went in under the reaching arms, to slash him just under the ribs and then straighten him again with a blow on the jaw.

It felt good, the hardness of bone meeting bone. Kindred had no idea who his opponent was, and it didn't matter anyhow. All that mattered was that this bastard had dared to lay a lusting hand on Judy Hazen. Blows reined on him but he scarcely noticed them. He ignored the excited yelling as the street began to came alive to fighting in front of the hotel. He did understand that this big ox didn't belong in a prize ring, however. He was relying on brute strength and a few dirty tricks he'd learned brawling around bunkhouses and trail camps.

One wagon-tongue right broke past Kindred's defense and closed up an eye for him, so that he had to shake his head to clear it of the sickening agony. Through a sheet of colored light he saw the bullet head, streaming blood, and without missing a beat he swung. He felt his knuckles split on hard, unyielding bone, heard the redhead's grunt of pain, and waded ahead. His next blow caught the man in the throat and sent him stumbling away from it, gagging. Kindred, about to hit again, saw him stagger and drop to one knee, both hands clutching his throat. He caught himself and waited, panting.

He was still standing over his opponent when somebody stepped in, shouldering him back. A smear of sunlight on a metal badge stabbed into his hurt eye and made it water.

Kindred dashed away the tears with the heel

of his hand, and recognized Cliff Johnson. The sheriff, for once, was not grinning his loose and meaningless grin. He achieved a scowl of some sternness and he was saying, 'Here! Here, now! We can't have this sort of thing! It just ain't what I'd expect from men of your position, Mr. Kindred! What do you suppose Mr. Roth or Mr. Hazen would think about it?'

'Roth?' Kindred paused in the act of staunching a trickle of nosebleed against his shirtsleeve. 'What's he got to do with this?'

'Why, Benteen here is his trail boss. Didn't you know?'

Kindred made both of his eyes focus and he watched the redhead climb back onto his feet. Benteen's face was a match for his own—bleeding from a torn cheek, and with a lip swelling. The sheriff looked from one to the other, disapproving, and he said loudly, 'By rights I should lock you both up. What was the row about, anyway?'

It was none of his business, nor any business of the dozen or so others who had gathered to the sight of blood like flies to honey.

'Personal matter,' Kindred said. 'Benteen knows what he did.'

Everybody looked at the redhead. He looked only at Kindred. Benteen's swollen mouth worked and twisted, but somewhere in the back of his head he must have realized what would happen if the truth about this fight came out.

77

'I made a little mistake,' he said hoarsely, and his own voice startled him.

Cold sober now, he was acutely aware of how bad a mistake it had been. These dudes didn't care what he did on Fremont Street, but no man, drunk or otherwise, molested a decent woman in a Western town and got away with it. Benteen had wits enough left to know this, and appreciate the danger he was in. He scowled defiance, but the next moment he whirled around and walked away from there.

Sheriff Johnson was breaking the crowd up, ordering it on. Kindred stooped for the hat that he'd lost in the fight. As he pushed straggling hair back and dragged the hat on, he found Judy beside him.

'Oh, Branch!' she exclaimed. 'Your poor eye!' She raised her hand as if she meant to touch his bruised face, then let it flutter down again. 'It's swelling almost shut.'

'Nothing a piece of raw beef can't fix,' he said shortly, because something else concerned him more. 'Tell me, Judy, did he hurt you any?'

'No. But it you hadn't come just when you did—' She drew in a shaky breath and then she directed a hearty glare toward the gallery. 'There are some men,' she said, 'who wouldn't even raise a hand to help a girl in trouble!'

For the first time, Kindred saw the man who stood at the top of the steps, tightly gripping the roof post. Blanched white, the man met

78

Judy's scorn with an expression of sick horror and utter shame. He opened his mouth as if to speak, but nothing came out.

The silence stretched. Kindred felt a numbness in him. His tongue lay in his mouth like a weight, but the thing had to be said. He swallowed, and he said heavily. 'Judy, this is your father.'

CHAPTER FIVE

Old Sam Hazen leaned forward in the rocker, his claw-like hands tight on its arms, his eyes furious. The glow from the setting sun, lying flat across the meadow and the yard, dyed his face and his crumpled body a hue close to blood red.

'Who did you say done this?' he demanded. 'Somebody belongin' to that damned Croyden Roth?'

Branch Kindred nodded. 'Trail boss. Name's Benteen, I understand.' He looked at Judy, wishing she hadn't blurted out the truth when the old man questioned her. He'd meant to pass over the injury to his face with some excuse or other, not mentioning the fight in Rock River, but Judy, out of her deep indignation, had insisted on telling everything. Only a frantic shake of Kindred's head had kept her from revealing Earl's ignominious part in the thing. That much, at least, she had held back.

Old Sam's clenched fist struck the arm of his chair.

'By God,' he said, 'I've had enough! Pass this word, Branch: Roth or nobody connected with him is settin' foot on Anchor grass for any reason at all! There's no room here for such scum!'

'Don't work yourself up, Sam,' Kindred said. 'After all, no real harm was done.'

'No harm?' Hazen snorted. 'No harm, when he dares to lay a hand on my girl, and my foreman has to use force to haul him off? We'll have no more of it. I've give my orders, you hear?'

'All right, Sam,' Kindred said.

The fierce energy suddenly drained out of Sam. His head dropped back, the chair creaking with his whole slumped weight. The sun was going, rapidly. It lay like a swollen drop of blood on the black hills westward, cut half in two now as it began to slide from sight. Shadows flowed across the flats. Sam's old face seemed to dim as the red glow faded. 'Judy,' he said, groping for her. When she laid her hand in his he closed on it fiercely. 'Thanks for comin' home,' he muttered. 'For spoilin' your visit, just to humor a foolish old man. Did— did Branch here tell you anything about—*why* I wanted you to come?'

'Yes, Gramps.' She caught Kindred's

warning look over Sam's white-thatched head. 'That is, he told me about my father—'

'I see. The old man nodded and closed his eyes. His voice was sinking almost to a whisper; passionate speech had drained his strength. 'Only smart, I suppose—prepare you for meetin' him. He ain't around just at the moment. Dunno when he'll be showin' up. Dunno what you're expecting—'

The voice droned off to silence. The fingers that clutched Judy's went lax. Kindred heard her gasp of alarm. Quickly he placed a hand on the old man's shirt, over his heart. The beat was there, steady enough, and relief touched him. 'Only asleep,' he muttered. 'It doesn't take much to wear him out these days.' He pulled up the blanket that lay across the wasted thighs, tucked it more securely about Sam. The sun had dropped from sight now and the porch was fading slowly into shadow.

Judy walked away. She went down the path to the gate and stood there clinging to the pickets, her head hanging—a small and pathetic figure. Kindred knew she was crying, and he went to stand beside her in the growing dusk. The cottonwood heads along the fence still swam in golden light above them, and at their backs a single window of the high second story gleamed brazenly.

Judy said, 'Oh, Branch! He looks so—*old*!'

'I know.'

She turned suddenly and laid her face

81

against his chest, and when he placed his arms about her he felt the sobs that made her body tremble. 'What if I should lose him?' she said in a smothered tone of fear.

'After all,' Kindred reminded her gently, 'you can't hold on to him forever, Judy. And remember, it isn't the way it would have been before. You won't have to be alone, now, whatever happens.'

He felt her stiffen. Abruptly she pushed away, raising angry eyes. 'You mean—him! You think I'd want anything from that man, after what he did today?' Her lips tightened. 'I said once already I hated him. And I didn't even begin to know!'

'You've got to be fair, Judy. He lacks the size to tackle a man like Benteen. Besides, he couldn't have realized you were his daughter.'

'Should *that* make any difference?' she cried.

'Whoever I might have been—for him just to stand by and do nothing, to let that—that—' She shuddered violently. '*You* wouldn't have, in his place. Don't try to make me think otherwise, just to make my father look better. My father!' she repeated, and her voice was sick with scorn.

She was in his arms again, her own arms tight about him, her young body pressed hard against him like that of a child seeking protection. 'Oh, Branch!' she sobbed. 'You've got to stand by me. Promise! Because, if—if anything happens to Gramps, it's *you* I'm going to need. You've been so wonderful to me. Always!'

And then her hands were behind his neck, pulling his head down. Her lips reached toward him, and fastened themselves against his mouth in a long and passionate kiss that was salt with her tears. Then she released him and ran up the path. Astounded and abashed, Branch Kindred watched her vanish into the darkening house. He raised a hand and slowly pressed the back of it against his mouth, and let it drop again.

He heard a bit chain jingle. Turning, he saw the horse standing motionless in the dusk beyond the gate. How long it had been there, he couldn't judge, but the storm of emotion reflected in the rider's pale face proved that he had seen and heard more than enough. Earl Hazen knew exactly what his daughter thought of him.

Branch Kindred waited.

The older man pulled himself straight, finally. 'Kindred,' he said huskily, and stopped. Whatever he meant to add would not be spoken. With a savage pull of the reins he jerked the horse about and made it jump with the spurs, heading it toward the corrals. Kindred could only watch him blend into the deepening shadows.

* * *

Croyden Roth paused at the door, hand on knob, and looked back at the man stretched out on the sagging hotel bed with an arm thrown across his eyes to shield them from the lamp. Roth's expression was sour. He waggled his hatbrim against his knee and said heavily, 'You're one pretty sight!'

'Go to hell,' Benteen growled. His lips were almost too painfully swollen for speech.

Roth's jaw hardened. 'See here, my friend! Don't you realize I'm trying to make an impression on this town? Another performance like the one you gave this after noon, any I might as well quit. Save that stuff for the cat-house on Fremont Street! What kind of men do you suppose people will think I have working for me, anyway?'

'I was drunk.'

'Yes, you fool, you were drunk! And do you know who the girl was that you tried to rough? Earl Hazen's own daughter!' His chest swelled in anger and disgust. 'By God, for a stupid mistake like that I'd haul you off that bed and thrash you myself—if Branch Kindred hadn't already done the job for me!'

That stung Benteen into lifting his arm away from his battered face. He half rolled up onto an elbow and glared at his chief. 'The hell with you!' he gritted. 'And that goes double for Kindred! Who does he think he is? Why, I can tear that monkey apart and one of these days

I'm going to! He took advantage of me. He come at me when I wasn't looking for a fight!'

'When you were too drunk for one, you mean.' Roth twisted the knob, jerked the door open. Just watch your step from now on. You've already killed what chance I had left at Anchor.'

Lamplight glinted red on the beard stubble on Benteen's bruised jaw. 'You never had any,' he said.

'Maybe not with the old man,' Roth conceded. 'But Earl Hazen is still worth working on—if I can manage to fix it up, that is, after what you tried with his daughter. It's just lucky I've got a better iron or two in the fire.'

He was still fuming as he dropped down the stairs to the dingy lobby. But, seeing Frank Chaffee at the desk, he put scowling anger away as if he were removing and pocketing a mask. The face the banker encountered, when he turned, was Roth's public front of dignified affability. Chaffee's rimless spectacles flashed lamplight as he bobbed a greeting. 'Ah, Mr Roth! I was just asking if you'd come in yet. Been riding again today?'

'Still looking around,' Roth agreed, shaking hands. They withdrew to a corner of the lobby and took chairs beside a dusty rubber plant. Roth brought out his cigar case and offered it to the banker, and they both lit up.

'Mrs. Marshall was in to see me this

afternoon, about a certain matter,' the banker said. 'I—er—had an opportunity to touch on the subject of your interest in the Dumont Lease.'

Roth was studying the fat man, reading his face like a page of print, while at the same time he kept his own expression carefully contained and unrevealing. 'Did the lady appear receptive?'

The banker smiled around his cigar. 'To speak quite frankly, Mr. Roth, I can't find that particularly important. She knows me for a business man who gives first thought to the bank's depositors. She knows that in any matter of a note extension, I have to take into consideration the sound business judgment of the person I'm dealing with.'

'And so you've given her some advice concerning the Lease?'

'I pushed the matter just as strongly as seemed wise.' The smile became a smirk. 'I'm quite sure she understands exactly what I think she ought to do.'

'Good,' Roth said. 'Very good.'

The fat man leaned closer, to lay a pudgy hand upon his sleeve. 'I make myself plain?' he said anxiously, lowering his voice, 'It would be well, I think, if at this stage you were to talk to Mrs. Marshall yourself. The sooner, in fact, the better.'

'I intend to,' Roth said, and they both rose. 'I'm anxious to settle this business, Mr.

Chaffee. I have a herd due within another day or so. I want to get it located—and,' he added, 'arrange my banking needs.'

The bald man nodded eagerly. 'You'll find me at your service, Mr. Roth.'

'I'm sure I shall,' Roth said. 'And I thank you again.'

He left the hotel and headed for the Marshall house.

⤴He knew exactly where it was located, having made a point of finding out very early in the game. It was one of the older houses of Rock River, gone a little shabby but marking the solid respectability of the late William Marshall's position in the town. Coming onto the porch, Roth could look through the colored glass of the front door panel and, beyond a half-open door at the hall's end, catch a glimpse of Gwen Marshall moving busily about the kitchen, clearing away after the evening meal. He watched her cross and recross the lighted opening, her hands filled with dishes and an apron about her slim waist. He saw her stop to untie a bib from around her little boy's neck and help him down from his chair. A handsome woman, he thought with a cool, impartial appraisal.

He turned the knob of the bell, then, and heard it echo through the rooms of the old house.

He had to wait only a minute or so. She came into the hall, minus her apron,

87

smoothing her skirts with shapely and capable hands as her heels tapped quickly toward the door. She placed a hand to her hair, a thoroughly feminine gesture. Then the door swung open, and she saw her visitor. Her eyes seemed to darken, her whole manner drawing in upon itself.

'You're Croyden Roth,' she said.

'Mrs. Marshall,' he said, and bowed, smiling. Without further words she stepped back, opening the door wider for him, and as he entered she took his hat and laid it on a table. She led the way through a tasseled doorway into a living room that was set with heavy, dark furnishings, a room which did not seem at all the proper background for her slight figure. She showed her caller to a chair and took her place on a horsehair sofa, where the glow from a lamp with a handpainted shade picked highlights from the black sheen of her hair.

Hands in her lap, shoulders stiffly straight, she faced the man and they talked of inconsequentials, a kind of sparring before the real purpose of his coming was broached. The little boy came into the doorway, and then trotted forward and crawled up onto the other end of the sofa and looked at Roth with his enormous brown eyes. Roth made some complimentary remark, which the mother pushed aside with an irritable gesture.

'Mr. Roth,' she said, 'I'm well aware this is

no social call.'

He inclined his head in agreement. 'No it isn't,' he admitted. 'Entirely. Though I see no reason why we can't place any dealings we might have on an open and friendly basis.'

'If it's all right with you, Mr. Roth, I prefer to treat business as such and nothing more.'

'Very well.' Allowing irritation to take some of the smoothness from his voice, he said briskly, 'I've been talking with Frank Chaffee about a tract of land known, I believe, as the Dumont Section. I understand you own this property?'

'I'm sure you know very well that I own it. You must also know that it has been under lease to Sam Hazen for nearly eighteen years.'

'Conditions change,' Roth reminded her. 'A new set of circumstances may arise that suggest new arrangement—seven after as long a time as eighteen years.'

She said, 'Mr. Hazen and my late husband were close friends. William Marshall had no need for grazing land. He bought in the Dumont property purposely to let Sam Hazen have the use of it, because Sam happened not to be in a position to buy it himself.'

'And I must say,' Roth assured her, 'that no one could carry friendship much farther than that.' He leaned forward in his chair, to add in a tone of great earnestness, 'But, Mrs. Marshall! There are closer ties. There is a man's duty to his wife and his son.'

The woman looked down at the hands that were twisted tightly together in her lap. She raised her head again. 'We're talking in circles, Mr. Roth. I know why you're here. Frank Chaffee made it clear that I could expect you. He made it even clearer that he wanted me to listen to what you have to offer. I'm sure he's told you that there is a matter of a note I can't meet, and that any hope of an extension rests entirely with him. Under the circumstances, naturally, I'm listening.'

Croyden Roth made a tsk-tsk noise. 'My dear young woman,' he murmured, 'I have no wish to bring pressure on you. The farthest thing from it,' he insisted, as she lifted her shoulders in a shrug. 'I've come to you because I think what I have to suggest is in the best interest of yourself and the boy. As for Sam Hazen, I would say that eighteen years of charity is enough for a man to expect of any friendship.'

'He has always paid a fair rent for the Dumont Lease!'

'But only fair,' Roth insisted. 'And now you need something more than that. It's a valuable property, and to be cruelly frank, you're in a position where you need every cent it can bring you. There's no point in pretending otherwise.'

He had got home to her with that. He saw it—that small significant slackening of defiance that was an admission of fine truth.

Some time dragged by before she answered, and then she said in a chastened tone, 'I suppose you want to buy the Lease?'

'As a matter of fact,' he said carefully, 'that's not exactly what I had in mind.'

This was the moment when he had to go slowly, had to remember that he had no money, and no cards in his hand beyond a busted flush. How convincing he could make himself sound in these next few minutes would determine just how far he could hope to get, with nothing to back him up.

'I have another idea,' he said, 'which might appeal to you more, since you don't seem too happy about the idea of selling. Perhaps you can understand that, from my point of view, this is an entirely new country—a new climate. I'll have to have more experience with it, learn more about it, before I'll be ready to tie up money here. What I had in mind to suggest was, that we try an arrangement on shares.'

Her surprise was obvious. 'Shares?'

'Let me explain. I have a herd on the trail, a thousand head that I'll need grass for when they arrive, sometime in the next day or two. Of this, about half is seed stock. The rest will be put on the market at the season's end. Now, I'd like to contract with you to let me hold my cattle on your graze and the adjoining summer range. I'll guarantee you an amount equal to the rental you would have had from Sam Hazen—*and*, in addition, a share in whatever

91

price I am able to get for the beef I sell in the fall. What that share will come to, will depend on the market, and on the vaunted ability of this range to put money fat on a herd. So, you see, if I profit as much here as I've been led to expect, you should come out very well indeed.'

The first signs of victory appeared immediately, and Croyden Roth congratulated himself. He had read the woman correctly, had know how near she was to despair. Now he saw indecision, that telltale first phase of yielding. Gwen Marshall rose restlessly, took a step toward the archway and another step hack, rubbing her palms together as if her hands were cold.

'I don't know very much about cattle,' she said, voicing an irrelevant objection. 'And I haven't even seen this herd of yours.'

'You're free to have it appraised when it arrives,' he assured her smoothly. 'And then we'll draw up the details of an agreement that will be suitable to us both. Also, I think I can guarantee that it will suit the bank as well. Chaffee as much as promised me that an extension of your note would follow as a matter of course.'

The woman stopped beside the table and laid a hand upon it. Light from the lamp washed up at her, revealing the pull of conflicting needs in her face. She glanced at the little boy, who was watching solemnly from his place on the sofa, and she drew a slow

92

breath.

'I'd like to think it over.'

'Naturally.' Roth came to his feet, and with his warmest smile he crossed to her and took her hand in both of his. 'Consult anyone you like. Get the bank's advice. I don't want to take advantage of the fact that this is a new sort of thing for you. I'd like, though,' he added, 'to have an answer as early as possible. After all, I can't put off making arrangements too long.'

She only nodded, still not looking at him. Croyden Roth dropped her hand. He said his good night and left her standing there. He got his hat and let himself out.

He knew an enormous satisfaction. Gwen Marshall could not hope to hold out, not under the pressures he could bring to bear on her. And, once in control of the Dumont Lease, he could move ahead as far as he cared to go. Neither Hazen nor Branch Kindred would be able to hold him back.

CHAPTER SIX

Tunneling rains had torn the banks of rotten snow to pieces. Now the sun was finishing the job, melting away the last clinging drifts until a man could almost see them sink into the earth. Hill slopes were alive with a music of many flashing little runs of melt water, and wild flowers showed their colors in sheltered, sunny places. Even the higher parks and meadows of rich summer graze would be open soon, ready for the gaunted herds from the grazed-out winter ranges along the Rock.

Anchor was in the final days of spring gather, with the cattle being loose—held in three large bunches in the lower hills. When the last of the calf crop had been dealt with these herds would be thrown together and then eased up onto the Dumont Lease and beyond that gateway into the higher grass, as it became available.

Such was the normal schedule, and the crew under Branch Kindred had done its work well enough. But things didn't *feel* right. Though little of it carried over into words, Kindred knew that a weight of uncertainty hung over his men. Old Sam's obvious ill-health, the note of discord brought by Earl Hazen's presence on the ranch, the formless threat that the stranger named Roth represented—none of these things was mentioned, but no one could entirely escape them.

It was probably this, and no real foresight, that gave him a premonition of new trouble that morning when Judy Hazen came riding up from headquarters. He was having a difference of opinion with a cow who'd tried to hide her calf from him in a clump of new-leafed aspen. Judy hauled Boots up at a distance to watch, greeting him with a wave of an arm which he was too busy just then to answer. The cow had her head down, ready to charge, and Kindred's wise pony moved around her carefully. Then a whoop and a sudden flash of coiled lariat in her face turned the cow aside and Branch Kindred went crashing into the brush around the base of the aspen clump.

The calf came popping out, bawling and frightened and streaking through the dappled light and shade. The cow gathered in her trembling offspring with a bawl that brought it straight to her, and after convincing herself that it was unharmed she seemed to forget her readiness to fight the man and the horse. Another yell from Kindred sent both cow and calf trotting away across the spongy, grassy open, in the direction he wanted. He hung his rope on the horn and turned to meet Judy as she rode up.

'They giving you trouble, cowboy?'

He returned her grin. 'Not too much,' he said but he sobered as he took in the engaging picture she made, astride the white-stockinged sorrel. There had been a subtle change in their familiar relationship of good spirits and friendly banter. The old moods no longer rested lightly on Judy. A disturbing gravity had replaced them, since her return from Montrose two days ago—since that scene on the hotel porch, in town, and the impulsive kiss she had given him. He suspected he was only

95

beginning to understand just what the kiss had meant to her, and it troubled him badly.

To hurt Judy Hazen was the last thing in the world he wanted. Yet, for a girl as young as she to form what she considered a romantic attachment for a man like himself could lead to nothing but hurt. Dimly, he understood the roots of it—the aftermath of her shocking experience with Jay Benteen, the contrast between her father's poor showing and Kindred's championing of her. It must have made a profound effect, and as a result she saw this man, whom she'd known for so many years, in an entirely new light.

He didn't know exactly what he could do about it.

'There's a letter,' she said, and took it from a pocket of her blouse. 'Gramps said I'd better bring it up to you.'

He remembered his premonition, then. The moment he first caught sight of her, he'd known that she brought bad news. He took the envelope, which had been brought to the ranch that morning by star route delivery, and when he recognized the handwriting he felt a jolt. But then he saw that, unlike others he had once received and treasured, this letter was not for him. It bore Sam Hazen's name. Face impassive under Judy's watchful frown, he drew out the paper from the envelope, unfolded it and read:

Dear Mr. Hazen:

I should like to talk to you at your earliest convenience concerning the property known as the Dumont Section, which you have been holding under lease from my late husband.

It is, I feel, a matter of considerable importance to us both.

Mrs. William Marshall

'What did Sam think about this?' he demanded.

'He seemed worried. He told me I'd better bring it right to you.'

Folding the letter, Kindred did some calculating and collided with a fact that he had almost forgotten: nearly three years had passed since the last renewal of the Dumont Lease. It was a matter no one on Anchor gave much thought to. Renewal had been an automatic thing, taken for granted. It had been this way all through the years Bill Marshall held the land, and even with his death it had never occurred to Branch Kindred that a change might come about. But something about this curt, businesslike note . . .

'You notice she doesn't say anything about renewing the lease,' Judy pointed out in a troubled voice. 'She just wants to talk about it.'

Kindred nodded, and folded the envelope and buttoned it away in his shirt pocket. 'So I'll go in and talk,' he said. 'Find out what's on her mind. This isn't at all what I'd expect from her.'

Judy put Boots alongside his roan, and they went after the cow and calf. They found the pair grazing on the new green blades that had sprung up from the soaked earth, and pushed them in the direction of the holding meadow.

The girl still had something weighing on her, and she rode in an odd silence for a space, Then she blurted out the question that Kindred had sensed was forming in her mind.

'A long time ago, Branch, didn't you and Mrs. Marshall—I mean, weren't you—' She faltered, confusion staining her throat and smooth brown cheeks.

'A long time ago,' he repeated, and smiled a little. 'All of three years. Yes, I suppose that would seem like a long time to you.' The smile turned grim, then, and he added, 'To me too, maybe!'

'But have you ever—that is, I mean—' She summoned up the courage to ask it: 'Do you still—love her, Branch?' Her voice sounded very small.

He glowered at the hands that held his horse's reins. He knew the answer she wanted, and he knew the one she feared. Being honest with himself, he couldn't truthfully say which was the true one. But Judy, seeing him hesitate, supplied her own.

'I think you do!' she exclaimed, and she

spurred ahead to hide her face.

When they reached the holding ground, he turned his cow and unbranded calf over to the men who worked around the fire and then proceeded to strip his riding gear and pile it on a fresh horse from the cavvy. Work was going forward smoothly. There were the smells of drying mud and woodsmoke and heated iron and blood and burning hair and flesh; the familiar sights and sounds of a working outfit at the labor of roundup. Yonder, remindful somehow of a spoiled and sullen boy, Earl Hazen stood with thumbs thrust into belt and watched the work, without seeming to take any part in it.

Hazen was a man at loose ends, owning no real place here and with no clear purpose since his plans to induce Sam to sell Anchor had battered themselves to nothing against the old man's iron will. He eyed Kindred with active resentment, but the foreman ignored him. They had exchanged no word since that moment two evenings ago when Earl had ridden up unobserved, and found Kindred and Judy together in the dusk.

Locating Ed Farrar, Kindred told him, 'I'm going to town. Something I have to see to. Keep the work going.'

Farrar nodded, frankly curious. It was a long haul, down to the river flats, but the foreman's manner didn't invite questions, and Ed didn't ask any. About to ride out, Kindred checked

99

his horse when he saw Earl walking over toward the place where Judy was patting Boots and slipping off the bridle so the horse could graze.

Judy's face lost its warmth and took on a sternness that stopped Earl Hazen. He raised a hand and would have spoken, but Judy stared at him as if he were a stone. Deliberately then she turned her back and went to the cookfire, where she proceeded to pour herself a tin cup of coffee from the big pot.

Earl Hazen stood alone, scorned and abandoned.

For just a moment, Branch Kindred felt something akin to pity, sensing a hurt and hunger in the man. After all, Judy was his daughter; and he could not make even the beginning of contact. Just then Earl Hazen seemed rather a pathetic figure. But after all, whom did he have to blame? Kindred reined his horse around and rode out, taking the downward trail.

Entering town, Kindred meant to ride straight to the mercantile, but he was hailed by a trio of men who stood under the awning of a feed store, conversing. They were John Drum and Will Spencer and Hank Laws, the first two being ranchers and neighbors of Anchor. Drum walked out into the sunshine and laid rope-scarred hands upon the hitching rack. Kindred pulled in and shifted his position in

100

the saddle, nodding a greeting. With no preiminary, Drum said, 'You know about it too, I guess.

'Know about what?' Kindred asked.

'Why, the herd that's coming in. Feed stock—three, four thousand head, they say—expected to hit Rock River before night. Rumors are flying all over town. That fellow Roth is supposed to be on his way now to meet them.'

Kindred said, 'Roth—'

'Damn it!' Drum's fist struck the chewed roughness of the pole. 'What does he think he's trying to do? This range already carries every head it will. Does he want to strip it clean?'

'Rumors have a way of growing,' Kindred reminded him. 'Maybe that's what this one has done.'

Will Spencer retorted angrily, 'What difference if it's four thousand head or four hundred? There's just no room! He hasn't any business bringing them in here. Where does he think he's going to put them? Up on our summer range?'

Laws, the feed store owner, made a sour face. 'Frank Chaffee and the Judge have been sucking up to Roth from the day he got here. A big shot with syndicate money behind him! Chaffee for one would give him the world for a chance to lay hands on some of it!'

'Maybe it's the guns in back of Roth,'

Spencer suggested, 'as much as the money. Maybe they're scared to give him less than he wants.'

'Benteen's a killer,' the merchant agreed, and wagged his head. 'He's got the sheriff buffaloed, for one.'

'And Johnson ain't alone. I sure as hell wouldn't want that cannon mad at *me*!' The rancher added, looking with respect at Kindred: 'But Branch here licked him, by God! The whole range has heard about it.'

'He was drunk,' Kindred said mildly.

'Just the same,' John Drum put in, 'Benteen ain't going to live that down soon. He knows it, and it gets home to him. I'm warning you, Branch, Jay Benteen's a vicious brute. Before this is over you may have to—'

His voice broke. His eyes shuttled past Kindred and his face lost its sternness and some of its color. Kindred saw the queasy way the other two acted and he shifted in his saddle to glance behind him.

A man had pushed through the doors of a corner saloon which stood just beyond a narrow side street. It was Jay Benteen. He came to the edge of the saloon steps and sunlight struck across his bruised and craggy features and revealed the leashed fury there. Sunlight made flame of his hair and sunlight shone too on the metal of the gun that thrust out of the cutdown holster sagging at his hip. Benteen's whole attention was on the man in

102

the saddle, but Kindred could almost smell the fear in Drum and Spencer and Laws as they wondered if the big redhead might have heard some part of what they had been saying. He couldn't repress a stirring of contempt.

He said, 'You wouldn't be trying to push me into a fight with him, would you, John? I'm not looking for one but I'm not backing away from it either. All I want is to do what's best for the brand I ride for. I don't want anyone else deciding for me what that is.'

The rancher opened his mouth to protest, but the words wouldn't come. All three of them looked wretchedly uncomfortable.

'Don't get us wrong, Branch,' Will Spencer said. 'Hell, we're all in this together.'

'If it really comes to a showdown,' Kindred said, 'I just hope you remember that, Will. I hope it very much.'

Benteen showed no sign of moving from his post in front of the saloon. He made no challenge. Kindred put a heel to his bronc's flank and set it on along the street.

At the mercantile he stepped down and tied, and walked into the store's half-gloom. There were no customers. At a rear counter Gwen Marshall was busy measuring yard goods. She straightened at the sound of Kindred's boots, and he thought she turned a little pale.

It was an awkward moment. They had exchanged scarcely a dozen words since Bill Marshall's death. They had never been

103

entirely alone; always the presence of the boy added restraint to their meeting. Now they both seemed to feel the lack of words to break through the distance that years, and Gwen's marriage to another man, had placed between them.

Gwen managed speech first. 'Hello, Branch,' she said, and didn't seem to know what to say next. Searching her face, he saw little change—a certain maturity, and a tiredness from the ordeal of recent experiences. He nodded gravely, his hat in his big, hard hands.

'Your letter came, Gwen.'

'Yes.' She wet her lips, and added on an indrawn breath, 'Let's go in the office. If we leave the door open I can tell when a customer comes in.'

The office was a tiny, uncarpeted room that still held the familiar smell of Bill Marshall's tobacco, mingled with that of the well-worn leather of the swivel chair and the other chair that stood beside the big roll-top desk. At Gwen's gestured invitation, Kindred seated himself and laid his sweaty hat upon his knee. She took the swivel chair, pushing aside an open ledger with a small movement of her hand. Looking at the ink-marked book, Kindred asked, 'Is business pretty good?' The atmosphere was still formal, still full of reserve.

'On the books,' she answered. 'Of course, in

104

cattle country a merchant's hard money comes in only in the fall. The rest of the year it's strictly a credit proposition.'

'I guess I never quite thought of it that way, Gwen. Wouldn't be surprised if you had to do a bit of juggling at times, keeping things balanced.'

'You do,' she admitted. 'And with all the expense since Bill passed on—well, that's why I had to write that letter.'

'You want to up the price of the lease? Sounds reasonable to me.'

'It's—not quite that.'

'Then what, Gwen? What are you trying to tell me?' He saw her fingers tighten and open, as she steeled herself to answer.

'I'm not going to be able to renew.'

A little clock on top of the desk ticked loud in the room's stillness. Kindred found breath trapped in his lungs and slowly released it.

'You've thought this out carefully?' he asked, at last. 'You've got good reasons, I suppose?'

'The best.'

'Sam has a right to know what they are, Gwen.'

'I'm planning to use the graze myself, Branch. I intend to feed cattle. On shares.'

Kindred waited but she said no more. She just sat there, rigid to the point of breaking with the strain of this scene. He himself was numb with disbelief, incapable of comprehending it, or knowing exactly what he should say. 'That's a mighty chancy proposition,' he got out finally. 'In a venture like that you could lose everything. You know nothing about the business.'

'I have a business partner who does. And Frank Chaffee thinks the idea is sound.'

'Chaffee?' It hit him then, like a sledging blow. He added up the things he had heard from John Drum and the others, and they tallied.

'Gwen, it isn't *Roth* you're dealing with?'

'What if it is?'

'But—you can't!' Kindred was on his feet, standing over her. He took a couple of paces to the door, swung back again. His hands clenched tight, the right hand mauling good hat brim felt. He was having trouble with his breathing. 'So that's where he plans to put that herd that's coming in!' he almost shouted. 'How many thousand head is it? Four?'

'Only a thousand,' she answered coldly.

'On a single section acre of graze!' He slapped his hat against his leg. 'Don't you understand? There'll be nothing to keep Roth from moving out from there, and helping himself to as much of the adjoining hill range as he wants!'

'What's so wrong with that?' Gwen Marshall demanded. She stood, bracing him like a man in the quiet of the office. Her face was dead white under its severe cap of black hair. 'It's all

106

free graze, isn't it?'

'But haven't you any thought for the fellows who are already using it? John Drum, Spencer, Barney Weil—they're every one of them friends and customers of yours, friends of Bill Marshall's! And yet you'd give Croyden Roth his foothold to shoulder the rest of them off the grass, clear out of the hills!'

'I don't understand you! A thousand head more or less can't upset things that much.'

'You think not? It all depends on the kind of man who would use those cattle—and gunmen like Jay Benteen—to grab off everything he can get his hands on. Roth's that kind of man, Gwen!'

He saw her eyes flicker; she knew he was telling the truth. But her mouth tightened resolutely and she put bite into her words. 'You seem to know a lot about what goes on in another man's mind, Branch Kindred! I see no reason to think Roth is the—the monster you make him out.'

'Because you don't want to see!' he retorted, really angry now. 'You've got some idea of all the money he's going to make you, and you've closed your eyes to the harm your greed will cause other people!'

Her breast lifted on caught breath. Pain rippled across her face, as if he had slapped her. 'Branch!' she cried hoarsely. 'No!'

There was a fury in him that couldn't be stopped. 'All right, I'll tell *you* something! I

107

won't stand aside and see the Hazens ruined. With the Dumont Section in his hands, Roth probably figures he can cut Anchor away from the best part of the summer graze. Well, when I'm ready I'll move our cattle across that section in spite of him! I'll give him a war, if he asks for it. I'll give him all he can use—and you'll back him at your own risk. Because, whatever happens, I'm looking out for Sam and Judy's interests!'

'Not your own interests at all, I suppose!' she came back at him, her voice cracking.

An odd hollow sensation took Kindred in the middle. 'What do you mean by that?' he asked slowly .

'Don't think I haven't noticed you with the girl? A little young for you, isn't she, Branch?'

He slapped her, hard.

The sound of it was a stinging, slashing sound in the stuffy room. Gwen staggered and the marks of five fingers appeared, red and burning, upon her cheek. They stood frozen, disbelieving, horrified by the thing that had passed between them. Then Gwen Marshall's eyes brimmed with the shine of tears. She shuddered with pain and humiliation and dropped her face into her hands.

'I'm sorry,' she said brokenly, the words muffled. 'I deserved that.'

'Gwen—' Agonized, Kindred stared down at her bent, dark head. Words struggled on lips that felt like wood, helpless to shape them, and

108

then he heeled around and walked at a long swift stride through the store building, and the door slammed its echo behind him.

Left alone, Gwen groped for the chair and let her trembling body into it. The first storm of weeping over, she laid her fevered cheek against the cool wood of the desk. Wide-eyed, yet sightless in a dank black well of shame and grief, she asked herself: What makes us say and do things as dreadful as this?

She knew the answer, knew it in her heart even if she would not admit it to her father. She loved Branch Kindred. She had loved him three years ago, when a deeply engrained hunger for the security she had never known had made her turn from him to William Marshall. And it was this guilty knowledge of her mistake that made her lash out at him now, made her blurt a thing she knew had no truth in it.

Well, to call him back and apologize for what she had said about him and Judy Hazen would have done no good. He would hate her, now, and it was no more than she deserved. A great despair overwhelmed her, made her conscious of the burden of anxiety and corroding care and the lingering shock of her husband's death. She sighed deeply and pushed herself up. She dried her wet cheeks on the palms of her hands and smoothed back her hair.

The mistakes had been made, and that was

that. Only one thing mattered now—Billy. In her fierce love for her child, she knew nothing must be allowed to interfere with the need to provide for him somehow, to give him the future that had become her sole charge. She must forget Branch Kindred. She must forget, too, his warnings about her forced relationship with Croyden Roth and what it could lead to. She didn't want to hurt Sam Hazen or Judy or anyone else. But there were times when you found yourself hopelessly backed into a trap, cornered and unable to move. So it was now with her.

She must think of Billy—only of Billy—and hold her resolution firm.

CHAPTER SEVEN

Riding home, Branch Kindred used his pony hard, while he was himself cruelly roweled by emotion and by a sense of impending disaster. He kept the bronc at a steady run, and only when the animal stumbled under him did he realize what his spurs were doing. A man usually careful of horseflesh, he checked himself at once, but the pony was dark with sweat when he came into the Anchor yard. By then his thoughts, ranging ahead, had already hit on the thing that had to be done.

With the entire crew on roundup,

headquarters appeared deserted; but by the time Kindred off-saddled and opened the corral gate to go in, rope in hand, and snare a fresh mount, Judy came hurrying down from the house. She took in the exhausted state of the pony, and of course that told her something had gone wrong.

'I didn't mean to push him so hard,' Kindred said before she could frame a question. 'Would you take care of him, Judy? I'm pressed for time.'

'Of course, Branch,' she said, and watched him worriedly as he settled on a gray that had good bottom and a long reach, and stalked it into a corner of the pen and expertly dropped his loop. When he led it outside Judy had the gate open for him, and she closed it afterward. He saw that her father had joined them. Earl leaned against a post of the corral, a cigar fuming in his mouth to match his mood, but he said not a word.

Kindred found a dry saddle blanket, lifted on the heavy stock rig that was still warm from the other bronc's back. As he cinched up with swift, practised movements he told the girl, 'I'm going into the hills again. May not get back tonight. If any of the boys drift in, send them up to me.'

'What's wrong, Branch? Is it something about the Lease?'

'We've lost it, Judy,' he answered solemnly. 'Gwen Marshall's turning the grass over to

Croyden Roth—to run a herd of feed stock he's bringing in.'

'She couldn't! Haven't we an option, or something?'

'Doesn't count. Roth's not leasing. It's a business deal, on shares. There's nothing we can do.'

Earl Hazen, who had listened to all this, said heavily, 'It would rather appear that you mean to do something.'

'I do,' Kindred snapped. 'I have no intention of waiting for him to lock the door on us, close us from our summer graze. I'm going to get our stock moved across that section while there's still time.'

'But it's too early,' Judy objected. 'That upper graze isn't open yet. We'll lose cattle.'

'It's possible. But, not as much if Roth has his way and closes Anchor away from its summer range. This is better than dying on the vine, Judy.'

Earl Hazen made an angry exclamation. 'When are you going to quit slandering him, Kindred? Roth wouldn't do such a thing to us!'

'That's your guess. I prefer not to tempt him.'

'And even supposing you were right,' Hazen insisted. 'So you get the cattle up there. How do you intend to get them down again, with the door closed behind you? Shoot your way out?'

'If I have to.' Kindred had every reason to

hold himself back, refuse to let this man grate him too hard, but it was a chore. Between Hazen and himself there existed a mutual irritation, a hostility that the man seemed determined to ride for all it was worth. Kindred found his hands knotted tight and he had to force himself to turn away from the man.

'I'll keep the crew working,' he told Judy. 'We should be able to get the stock moving by early tomorrow morning. I Judge Roth will be giving us that much time. It's all we'll need.'

'And supposing a late blizzard hits the mountains tomorrow night?' Earl Hazen demanded with brutal directness. 'And wipes us out?'

The gray was ready. Kindred swung astride. 'While I'm ramrodding this outfit,' he said, 'I'll have to do whatever I think is best. That's how it is, Hazen.'

As the horse started forward Judy touched his knee and said, 'Be careful, Branch!' He smiled at her, nodding, but the gray had carried him only a few yards when she called out, 'Wait! I want to come with you!'

He twisted in the saddle and saw her running to catch him. 'No. You're needed here, Judy—with Sam. I'll see you tomorrow.' Before she could argue, he swung a hand in farewell and lifted the gray into a lope.

Earl Hazen stood motionless, filled with a cold and crawling dislike.

While I run this outfit . . . The arrogance of the man! Just who did he think he was? A nobody—a heavy fisted tough come from nowhere to batter his way to the post of foreman of a ranch like Anchor, and win over an old man's blind trust and his agreement in any decision or move he cared to make! Hazen thought of their first meeting, and he could almost feel that fist slam again into his cheek, throwing him against the wall of the flimsy foreman's shack. He raised a hand and touched the place, and he smoldered inside.

He watched his daughter take down a rope from the gatepost, slip it over the neck of the lathered horse Kindred had left in place of the gray. She slapped the sweated neck, an absent, friendly gesture, and then walked away toward the barn leading the animal. Doing Kindred's hostler chores, Hazen thought darkly, and glad to do them! She'd polish his boots if Kindred asked her. While he himself—her own father—could do nothing at all to please her, or make her give him more than the most perfunctory cold attention. All right, he was to blame for that. Considering everything, perhaps it should take it for granted that she had little use for him. But he would make amends, given a chance. If it hadn't been for Kindred's presence he could have made progress by now toward a reconciliation.

Kindred. Always Kindred! Ruining any hope of the sale he might have been able to talk his father into, and the commission Croyden Roth had all but promised if it went through! And now, in spite of every warning, deliberately pushing Anchor along a reckless course that could end only by making an enemy of Croyden Roth, and destroying all the good will Earl Hazen had worked so hard to build with him.

Unless . . .

With the thought, came the certainty that it was the thing that had to be done. For just a moment he backed away from it, a trifle dismayed—and then he knew he had made his decision. He tossed his cigar aside. With almost frantic haste he caught up and saddled a horse. Afterward, riding over to the house, he dropped reins at the gate long enough to hurry inside and take his bat and a leather brush jacket from the rack of hooks inside the door. Starting out with these, he heard the anxious voice of his father calling from his rocker beside the window.

'What's going on out there? Where's Kindred off to?'

Earl halted. Impatience and that roiling mood roughened his tongue. 'Kindred? Why, he's off to finish the wrecking of this ranch, that's all! You want to know what's happened?' he went on, walking around to plant himself in front of the old man. 'Croyden Roth—the man I could have got you a good price out of for this iron—Roth has turned around and taken

115

over the Dumont Lease. And what do you think of that?'

Sam's face drained slowly until it became a waxen death mask. The blue eyes bulged. The hands that clutched the arms of his rocker began to tremble. 'No!'

'Where do you think it leaves Anchor?' his son shouted. 'Just sit there and figure—and then think about the chance you could have had to sell if you'd only listened to me!'

'Listened to *you*?' The old man's jaw jerked spasmodically. 'And who else was it lost me the Lease, in the first place? By God, thanks to you I'm right back where I was eighteen years ago!'

Earl took a step toward his father, and a tremulous breath swelled his lungs. 'Still throwing that up to me? Still condemning me because of something I did that long ago? All right! Let Kindred do what he likes. Let him shove our cattle into the hills before it's safe! I know what *I'm* going to do!'

He strode toward the door, wrenched it open. Behind him his father cried, 'Wait! Come back here! Where do you think you're going?' Heedless, he slammed outside as Sam came out of the chair, supporting himself feebly on shaking arms. The old man uttered his son's name, but it was little more than a hoarse croak.

Earl Hazen, already half way down the walk from the house, didn't even hear it. Vaulting the gate, he flung himself into saddle, swinging the horse and feeding it the spur for a lunging start that nearly unseated him. When the animal settled, Earl put him at a hard pace on the trail to town. He rode down the slant of this range at the edge of the hills, and the sun sank in a crimson smear and the earth lay hushed as daylight faded. Color left the land, and smoky dusk poured in to take its place.

When he brought the town into sight, lamps were already burning in the houses and another fire blazed yonder on the flats, where Rock River made a ribbon of beaten steel against the darkening earth. Hazen could see cattle moving blackly, feeding along the river, closeheld by circling riders.

Entering town, he found an unmistakable overtone of excitement and tension in the air. Men gathered in the shadows along the building fronts, earnestly talking. Hazen had made no friends and few acquaintances since his return, and he drifted on along the street, scanning faces for one he knew well enough to ask a question. He rode as far as the jail— almost to the turnaround that fronted the stage station at the foot of the long street— before he made a connection.

Cliff Johnson's figure was limned faintly by the glow of light from beyond barred windows, as he stood there in the dusk before his office door. Hazen pulled rein and leaned forward in the saddle to ask, 'Any idea where I can find

Croyden Roth, Sheriff?'

The officer jerked his head toward the flats beyond town. 'That's Roth's trail herd out there. I reckon he's with it.' The sheriff's gruff voice lacked good humor; there was an air of worry about him. 'I hope he ain't gone and done nothing that's going to lead to trouble. I've heard some pretty hard talk about any more cattle being brought in on this range.' He shook his head, frowning at the troubled run of his thoughts, but Earl Hazen didn't bother to answer. He straightened and touched the horse with his heel. Making a turn beyond the stage station, he took the trail that would lead him out onto the flats.

Stars were pointing up the soft velvet sky. Behind him, a rising moon made a brilliant spreading glow above the sharp-cut outlines of the mountains, but it hadn't yet broken above their high barrier. Out ahead, as Hazen drew nearer, cattle-sound became more audible on the breeze that stirred along the river. The fire leaped higher and shone on the canvas of a chuck wagon parked beside it. Silhouettes of men moved blackly there. And now three riders, coming at a drumming lope along the trail, slowed as they saw a lone figure approaching.

Earl Hazen said uncertainly, 'Mr. Roth?'

They pulled rein. He could sense the stares that searched him in the near-darkness. Saddle leather popped as a mount shifted its hoofs in the short grass and the man at Hazen's left said harshly, 'Let's see your hands. They better be empty, mister!'

Quickly he lifted them away from his body, to show he had no gun. Croyden Roth, the center of the trio facing him, demanded, 'Who is it?'

He gave his name. As he spoke he heard the sputter of a sulphur match and the man who had challenged him held the flaming stick high. Its light played briefly, showing Hazen this stranger's narrow, hatchet-thin face, and on Roth's other side, the craggy-featured Jay Benteen. The one with the match said, 'You know this jasper, boss?'

Roth gave a nod. 'All right, Bart. It's the man I told you about.' The match had burned down and the rider who held it cursed as it bit his fingers, letting it drop in a bright red arc that went out as it reached the ground. Roth continued pleasantly, 'Earl, this is Bart Hooker. He just brought in a herd for me.'

Hazen did not much like the appearance of this Hooker. He looked liked another Benteen, and Earl had already had his fill of that one, the day Benteen roughed the little girl who later turned out to be Judy. He wished, uneasily, that Roth could do without such men on his payroll. Still, Roth was a big operator and he must know how to handle his own business. Hazen said only, 'Seems like a good-sized bunch of cattle.'

'A thousand head, all in good shape.' Roth was in a genial mood. He kneed his horse forward and Earl Hazen, turning his mount, fell in at Roth's stirrup. The four of them drifted on like that over the dark flats, the lights of town growing larger ahead. The moon had pushed its way above the high horizon, fading the stars as its glow spread out across the sky.

'I heard you were planning to put your cattle on the Dumont Section,' Hazen ventured.

He saw Croyden Roth incline his head in a nod. 'Yes, I'm afraid that's how it is,' Roth agreed, in a faintly regretful tone. 'I had to make some kind of a deal. I couldn't wait forever for the old man to see the light.'

'Sure. I understand,' Earl said, and added quickly, 'But I haven't given up hope.'

'I don't know. It looks doubtful. Your father plainly intends to listen to Kindred, instead of you.'

Mention of the name tightened Hazen's throat, like a bitter taste. 'Kindred,' he said harshly, 'is going to fall on his face, one of these days. Do you know what he's up to now?' he went on, blurting it out with a heedless rush. 'He figures to risk shoving Anchor's beef clear up into the hills, clear above snow line, before you've had time to settle this herd of yours. Tomorrow morning, he plans to do it.'

'You mean he'd run them across the

Dumont Section?' Roth's head swiveled fast. Hazen could almost feel the searching stare burn into him, in the moonlit darkness. And then, in an altered, quieter tone Roth said, 'Just why are you telling me?'

Now that it was done, and the words said, Earl Hazen knew a quick, uncomfortable prodding of conscience, almost of guilt. Why, indeed, must he be in such a lather to betray Kindred's plans? Was his hatred of his father's foreman really this strong?

But he downed such disturbing doubts, remembering an argument that had sounded valid the first time he put it. 'Why, it's a crazy thing he's trying. Early as it is no one can count on the weather in these hills. Kindred could lose us every head of stock we own!'

And if Kindred can be stopped, he thought, working stubbornly at his own self-justification, then without summer graze Anchor will be in no position to continue operating. Dad will have to sell. Naturally, he doesn't want to. But in his state of health, it will be the best thing in the world for the old man, just to get the weight of it off his shoulders. He'll see I'm right . . .

They came into town, then, and as their horses pulled four abreast into the long main street Croyden Roth said, 'Kindred may be in for a little surprise. Benteen, locate Judge Gore for me—he lives on that side street, a block north of the hotel. Tell him I want him.

He'll find me at the jail, with the sheriff. I'm damned if anybody's pushing cattle across land I hold a claim to!'

CHAPTER EIGHT

Cinching up, Branch Kindred felt cold moisture strike the back of his hand. He paused to examine the spot, apprehension knotting up inside of him. He expected to find a snowflake melting against his skin but it was nothing more than the fine, early morning mist that swirled about him. The fog threaded whitely along the draws, laid gray fingers through the pines, obscured the ridges. It gathered on the shaggy winter pelt that his pony hadn't shed yet. It made a white plume in front of Kindred's face as he let out a long, slow breath, moving methodically to finish knotting the latigo in the chill cinch ring.

Sounds were muffled by the mist—the grumbling of the men as they broke camp, the stir of cattle in the gather. Ed Farrar came tramping over with his jacket buttoned high around his throat, hands shoved deep in pockets. He said gruffly, 'Ought to be ready to move out in another half hour.'

'Good,' Kindred said. 'You know where to pick up the other bunch. Just hold them together and keep them coming.

Farrar scowled darkly. 'We may need snowshoes before this day's work is over.'

'It's not as bad as that,' Kindred said, and swung into the saddle. 'I'm going to scout as far as the Lease. If everything's clear I'll ride back and meet you.'

He moved away into the fog, and its white tentacles gathered him in and its dank breath enveloped him.

Last night the stars had hung like lamps in a black velvet sky, and the moon had silvered rocks and trees and brush until you needed no firelight to see what you were doing. Certainly there'd been no indication of what they would waken to this morning. But such was the way of this country at this season of the changing year. Down on the flats the sky was probably clear and turning bright and warm with dawn. Higher—above the Dumont Section, in the upper parks and mountain meadows—this bank of cloud that engulfed the mountains could have brought with it a sizable fall of snow. The thought pinched Kindred's mouth down hard.

Earl Hazen had offered no idle warning. This was still too early to trust a herd to that upward country, where winter had not completely loosened its grip. Yet he'd named the play as best he saw it, and even in the face of a turn in the weather he could only play it out. Should he fail, should the risk prove bad, he had no doubts as to what it would mean.

123

Earl Hazen could demand his scalp, then, and get it. Worse than that, with a loss of cattle Anchor itself stood to face ruin—and Sam and Judy with it.

But grimly he pushed ahead.

He climbed steadily. The strengthening daylight grew scarcely any brighter. The dripping trees and crowding ridges hemmed him in, the dark green of pine beginning to give place now to the more brilliant, shaggier fir. A fine rain spun out of the low cloud ceiling and it felt icy cold where it struck and stung his face. He pulled his hat brim lower.

Though he tried not to, he kept returning hopelessly, again and again, to that scene yesterday in the mercantile—to Gwen Marshall, and himself, and to the thing that time had done to them. He'd been over it often enough, during the hours since; it was a weary and useless treadmill that trapped his plodding thoughts and held them prisoner. It got him nowhere at all.

He didn't know, really, that she had ever cared for him three years ago in anything like the way he had felt about her. He had dared to think she did, but surely he must have been mistaken. He'd never spoken for her hand, of course. As merely another puncher on the Anchor payroll, he'd had little enough to offer a girl—even one as little used to luxury as Milt McCune's daughter. But he knew she'd understood his feeling for her, and there had been certain tender moments that made one whole spring a time of sweet memory that clogged his throat, even now. And yet, always there had been that reserve—that withholding of something, that drawing back. Never once had she said she loved him. Instead, there came a day when she'd cried and fled from his clumsy attempt at lovemaking. He'd sensed then that she was confused, afraid of him— afraid of the hardship and heartache to which life with Milt McCune had betrayed her mother. It was understandable that she'd want something more, a security that he couldn't have offered.

He hadn't pressed her. He'd stayed away, giving her a chance to settle her thoughts and emotions. And then only a day or so after Sam named him foreman, with the hike in pay that would have made it possible to speak to her— word had come that she was pledged to marry Bill Marshall: A man with a business, with money; a man who could take care of her and of her shiftless father in the bargain. Well, Kindred tried to tell himself, she'd showed what she really wanted. The differences in ages had apparently meant little to her. It was, he realized suddenly, not a lot more than the difference that existed between himself and Judy Hazen. And in the face of that, Gwen had had the nerve to say . . .

Kindred sighed miserably. It did no good to hash something over and over. It did no good to hate himself for that unbelievable moment when his hand struck her. He looked at the hand now, lying along his thigh, and he clenched it hard. To think that they would ever come to this! But how could he have believed, either, that a pathetic need for security could have grown into the kind of greed that would let her ally herself with a man like Croyden Roth?

He could make allowances for everything but that.

Somehow he forced this dark run of reflections from him, closing the door on the past, concentrating, on the job he had to do now and the gamble he was taking with Anchor's very future. Slick faces of flatiron rock lifted eerily in the fog. Earth movement had left acres of this tilted granite, that served as a fence between Sam Hazen's graze and the upper meadows and left him reliant on the Dumont Lease as the one way to get into them. In earlier days, before he came into control of the Lease, Sam had worked on a fairly small scale, utilizing the few pockets of summer graze that were then available. Since that time he'd twice expanded the scope of his operations. Those pockets would now hold, at the most, a third of the beef that carried his brand. And with such an investment, there could be no abrupt retrenching. Either a way had to be kept open for the bulk of his stock to reach the better graze beyond the tilt-rock barrier, or Sam faced ruin. It was as simple as that.

That essential gap was a narrow one, scarcely a quarter mile wide, and just behind lay the section of land old Jake Dumont bad claimed and patented. Dumont had been a hermit—more than a little crazy, some thought. Kindred couldn't hold with them. At least, he had certainly known good graze when he saw it. Coming in between the mule ears of rock that guarded the entrance, Kindred drew rein and peered across the empty acres of deep grass, so rank and rich it seemed almost to grow faster than a steer could eat it.

There was water, too, a small jewel of a lake steaming grayly beneath the low cloud ceiling. Numberless springs born of melt water fed the lake, runneling musically through the surrounding pasture. Clumps of pine and fir crested the rises that thrust up here and there across the bottom of the cup. At the far end the ground lifted more sharply, into a fringe of timber that led on toward the fastness of the higher hills. And the spires of those yonder trees, he saw, were frosted now with the white of new snow.

He frowned at them, asking himself whether there had been only snow enough to cover the trees, or if the drifts were deep underneath— in which latter case it would be folly to think of taking cattle into them. But you couldn't tell at this distance. He kicked his bronc ahead, flanking a spur of rock, and brought into view the cabin old Dumont had built for himself, three years ago. It had been built to last, to stand against all weathers, since the old hermit had even spent his winters alone here, trapping and hunting. Anchor used it still, as a summer line camp.

A whiff of woodsmoke, brought to him on a vagrant shifting of the wet wind, spoke its warning even before he saw the horses in the corral beyond the cabin, or noticed the curling blue ribbon above the stone chimney. Before he could react, a voice somewhere in the rocks he had just skirted said, 'You've come far enough!' A rifle hammer snicked back as a thumb cocked it.

A shock ran along Kindred's nerves. The gray must have felt his quick tension, for it made a move to bolt. But he knew danger when he saw it and he held the animal under a tight rein. He heard bootleather scrape against stone. The voice at his back—one he didn't think he had ever heard before—told him in a tone of curt satisfaction, 'I'm glad you're gonna use your head. I've had a cold wait up here and I ain't feeling too good about it. How many more with you?'

'Figure it for yourself,' Kindred said.

'I figure none,' the sentry answered promptly. 'You come in to me like a man all alone, expecting nothing. If I'd had an itchy trigger finger I could have picked you off any time in the past five minutes. I see you got a gun under the skirt of that blanket coat,' he added. 'Reach over with your left hand and drop it on the ground. Careful! Keep your right hand where I can see it.'

Kindred obeyed. He got the windbreaker unfastened and pulled the gun. It thudded on the ground beside his pony's rear hoof, and the nervous animal side-stepped away from it.

'Good,' the man said. He levered his rifle and fired twice in the air.

Hard on the heels of the signal, the door of the cabin flapped open and men came rushing out. A couple hurried toward waiting horses, leaped astride and spurred up across the boggy meadow, circling the end of the lake. They seemed to grow rapidly in size as they neared.

Kindred counted at least eight men down there. About half were moving now, more slowly than the first pair had done, to get into saddles and come quartering across the spongy meadow. Their numbers confirmed a dark truth that filled Branch Kindred's mind. He said over his shoulder to the rifleman, 'You were waiting for me. How did you know?'

'Oh, we had a tip. Roth has his ways of finding out what he needs to.'

'Who told him?'

The only answer he got was a chuckle, and the dry comment: 'You want to take it easy, mister. You'll live longer. That is, if you stay out of Croyden Roth's way.'

The first pair from the cabin were pulling up now. One was Cliff Johnson, the sheriff. Kindred didn't know the other. He saw a narrow face with a Roman nose too big for it, and a pair of eyes as cold and deadly as the sixgun that dropped level on Kindred's chest.

'This him?' the hawk-faced stranger asked. 'This the one we're looking for, Sheriff?'

Johnson nodded. He seemed to have trouble meeting Kindred's eyes directly. 'Yeah. This is Kindred, foreman at Anchor.'

The hawk-faced man called to the sentry up in the rocks: 'Anyone with him?'

'No sign, Bart.'

'It figures,' Bart said. 'They'll be moving the cattle slower than a man riding alone. No trouble yet, I guess.' But the gun muzzle stayed on Kindred's chest. 'So you're Branch Kindred. A pretty tough ramrod Sam Hazen has, they tell me. You even licked Jay Benteen.'

'I can't lick a gun stuck in my face,' Kindred said pointedly.

'You suggesting I take you on?' Bart smiled a little, a meager warping of the thin-edged scar that was his mouth. 'Sorry, Kindred. Hand-to-hand is Benteen's department.'

'And this is yours?'

The man with the rifle said, 'It's Bart Hooker you're talkin' to, friend. That name mean anything to you?'

'It will after this morning.'

130

He hadn't heard the name before, but he couldn't be mistaken about the type. This Hooker was as dangerous as Jay Benteen. But Benteen reminded Kindred of a club, while this hawk-nosed killer suggested a sheathed rapier. He was all sharp intelligence and supple cunning. Somehow Hooker and Benteen reflected two sides of Croyden Roth's dark nature. The fact that two such as these took orders from Roth increased Kindred's respect for his enemy.

'We're wasting time,' Bart Hooker said to Cliff Johnson. 'Give him the paper, Sheriff.'

The lawman reached into an inner pocket of his coat and brought it out—a legal-looking document which he handed to Kindred.

'It's an injunction,' he said. 'Legally drawn and signed by Judge Gore, at the request of Croyden Roth. It forbids you to bring any cattle onto this section of land.'

Kindred didn't even glance at the paper. 'Roth doesn't own this property, Sheriff.'

'He has a commitment. The Judge saw fit to issue the injunction. It's my duty to enforce it.'

'We all know you take your orders from Gore,' Kindred said. 'And now it's obvious where Gore is taking his. He'd side with any man who's out to break Sam Hazen. Well, the hell with both of you! I've got a crew coming up with a herd that has to get across into the hills yonder. That's open graze, and this is the only feasible route we can take to reach it.

131

Roth has to give us passage.'

A faint sheen of sweat highlighted Johnson's cheekbones. 'Not according to the terms of that injunction,' he retorted doggedly. 'If you don't like them you can take it up with the Judge.'

'I may, yet.' Suddenly Kindred's hand balled, crumpled the document and flung it away. 'But I won't do my arguing with papers!'

He saw the man stiffen. 'With bullets, then? Take my word for it, you'll buy nothing but trouble. You're dealing with the law!'

'And with a hell of a lot of law,' Bart Hooked added. Casually he flipped aside the unbuttoned brush jacket he wore, and Kindred saw the dull gleam of metal pinned to the shirt beneath. 'As of last night I'm a deputy sheriff of this county. So are the rest of these men— all of us duly and legally sworn. We'll stop your herd by any means you force us to use. And if you push this to a showdown, Kindred, you nor Anchor will ever hear the last of it.'

Kindred looked past Hooker at the rest of the men, who had come up now and were sitting their horses a little distance away. Tin stars pinned to every one of them, by God!

He said, 'Nothing halfway about you, Cliff. When you and the Judge sell out, you do a real thorough job of it.'

Johnson flinched exactly as if he had been hit. 'Damn you!' he said. 'You can push me too far! I'll forget what you just said, if you turn your cattle back and keep them away from here. Defy an injunction and I'll promise you all the trouble you ask for!'

It was an ultimatum. It left nothing more to be said. Kindred felt the finality of it, but he hung on for a long and pregnant moment, knowing he had no answer, yet unwilling to back down. And then Bart Hooker shifted his weight in the saddle and his narrow mouth drew up in a wicked, V-shaped smile. Very softly he said, 'You're trespassing, mister.'

Kindred jerked the reins. As he turned, he saw the dull gleam of the rifle slanted down at him from the tumbled pile of boulders. The barrel swung, the hidden guard covering Kindred and following him carefully as he moved past at a slow walk.

Then a word from Bart Hooker made him hold up. 'Just a minute!' The gunman rode forward, holstering his sixgun, while Kindred waited. He leaned far out of the saddle and his long arm reached the weapon the Anchor foreman had thrown down. He came up with it, rolled out the cylinder, shook the cartridges from it and flung them away. He snapped the empty cylinder back in place. 'Your gun,' he said, and tossed it at its owner.

Kindred plucked the weapon out of the air and shoved it into holster. He rode out, and this time only silence followed him.

* * *

133

Ed Farrar held the reins close and stared at his boss in dismay and unbelief. Below where they sat, Anchor beef plodded slowly up a long and brush-rimmed draw—red-and-white shapes, drifting against the straight trunks of the wet-darkened timber. The high mist was breaking, letting an almost colorless light sift down through fir needles to touch the faces of the men but not warm them.

Farrar stammered, 'You said we *what*?'

'Take them back,' Kindred repeated drearily. 'We're closed out of the Lease. Roth has bought the law. They're waiting for us up there, with guns and deputy badges and a piece of paper that's stronger than all the rest put together. We can't fight that kind of odds.'

The puncher's eyes kindled a dangerous light. 'There's nine of us,' he reminded Kindred.

'And just as many of them. Besides which, they have nothing to lose in a fight.' He shook his head. 'No, Ed. We're stopped. We buck Judge Gore's sheriff and that court order, and Anchor's done for.'

'It's done for anyway, with no graze for these cattle.'

Kindred wiped his sleeve across his face, a gesture of total resignation. 'Take them back,' he said for the third time, and lifted the reins. 'There's nothing else for it.'

'Branch—'

134

He half-checked the roan, hearing all the disappointment, the hurt baffled puzzlement in Farrar's voice.

'Who was it, Branch? Who do you suppose could have tipped them off, what we meant to try and do?'

'I know who it was,' Kindred said heavily. 'I can hardly believe it even now—but God help me, I know.'

And as he rode down the slants, not answering the startled hails of Anchor crewmen who saw his dark expression as he passed, the one unbelievable thought kept repeating itself in his stunned consciousness: Gwen! Did you really think that you—even you—could do this to the Hazens and not answer for it?

He felt as though something in him had sickened and died.

CHAPTER NINE

Long before he reached Anchor, the clouds had rolled back and been drawn away to streamers of mist under the heat of a strong sun. Cottony layers still clung to the high peaks but the day had turned out a blue and beautiful one, and Kindred knew the unmistakable truth.

'If he had only been able to cross the Lease,

135

he would have won his gamble. Winter was truly over.

You could tell from the very feel of the air, from the winey warmth that lay upon the earth. Under that sun, another few days would see the higher meadows fully opened up to grazing. But it would do Anchor no good, now.

It was a bitter knowledge to take with him, piled onto the shock of Gwen Marshall's betrayal. This, he still could not understand. Could greed really weigh so strongly on her? Or had she done this out of spite, taking it out on Sam and Judy for that scene in the office? He couldn't believe it; he just couldn't. She hadn't changed so much in a few short years. He couldn't have been that much mistaken about her . . . could he?

He came into Anchor headquarters and found it utterly silent under the warm, midday sky. He rode directly to the main house, dismounted before the gate and walked up the path. The front door opened and Judy came out.

She watched him, her face drained and white and old. She spoke his name, brokenly. Then she ran down the steps and into his astonished arms.

'Oh, Branch!' she sobbed. 'How awful!'

Bewildered, he could only stand and hold her with an awkward gentleness. 'I don't understand,' he said. 'Judy, how on earth did you know?'

She drew back. 'Know?' she echoed. 'Branch, it's Gramps!'

He rushed past her and into the building. An utter quiet chilled him. Across the small living room, the door of the old man's bedroom stood open. Kindred walked over there, and on the threshold he halted and fumbled off his hat.

For an unmeasured length of time he stood gazing at the motionless form upon the bed, the closed eyes, the folded hands. In life, Sam Hazen had never given an impression of utter fragility. In death he seemed so frail and wasted, so . . . damned pathetic.

Kindred pulled himself out of the dark depths and drew a long, slow breath. 'When, Judy?' he called.

'In his sleep,' she answered at his elbow. 'He never woke. When I called him this morning—' She was crying, silently, a small fist pressed against her mouth. Kindred put his arm around her shoulders.

'Sam was an old man,' he reminded her gently. 'He knew it could come any time.'

Judy raised her head, in blind grief. 'But, to spend his last evening like that—upset and anxious about the turn in the weather, worried at the thought of what you might be running into—'

'Judy! You didn't tell him about the Lease—and what I meant to do?'

'No, Branch! Of course not!'

'But then, how—'

The faint creaking of a tread in the staircase brought his head around. Earl Hazen had come halfway down, moving almost without sound. He stood there peering at the man and the girl, and he looked white, sick. Suddenly Kindred knew.

Dropping his hand from Judy's shoulders, he walked slowly toward the stairs. He kept his voice low but it lashed whiplike in the stillness. 'It was you,' he said. '*You* told him. Were you deliberately out to kill the old man?'

'Why, damn you!' Earl Hazen came down the rest of the way, his hand white-knuckled on the bannister. He faced Kindred at the foot of the stairs, and his lips barely moved in the stiff mask of his face as he hurled his answer. '*I* wasn't the one who wanted to risk the ranch and every head of beef we owned, pushing our stock into the hills before it was safe! Certainly I told him! It was time he knew what kind of a fool he had for a foreman!'

With a cry Judy denied it all. 'Gramps knew you could always be counted on to make the best decision. He never once last night said that what you intended doing was wrong!'

'This isn't necessary, Judy.'

'It certainly isn't!' A gleam of jealousy had kindled itself in the hot anger of Earl Hazen's eyes. 'I'm sick and tired of seeing you run to this man. I'm your father!' I think it's time you realized that!'

138

'What makes you think I don't realize it?' she lashed back at him. 'I get so ashamed sometimes I could—'

'Don't,' Kindred said, quickly. 'Don't! You musn't!'

Earl Hazen's harsh voice cut across his own. 'Kindred, I'll handle my own family difficulties. There's just one thing I want you to do. Get your stuff together and get off this ranch. You're fired!'

Very slowly, hearing Judy's shocked gasp Kindred turned back to the man. His hands knotted tight and he could feel the bite of the nails into his palms.

'What makes you so sure,' he said, 'that it's for you to say? What gives you the idea Sam would have left this ranch to you?'

Earl Hazen's mouth twisted, mockingly. 'A lot of good it would do him to try and cut me out! It so happens Judge Gore and I reached an understanding on that, just last evening—'

'You saw Judge Gore last night?'

The truth hit Kindred then, with a rush. There was an element of soul-deep relief in the knowledge that he had been wrong in his suspicion of Gwen, but loathing and contempt quickly swamped it. 'So it was you! After telling Sam enough to start him worrying and lead him to a stroke, you sold us out! I ought to have guessed! It's just like you!'

Hazen lost his assurance. His face went almost comically blank at the knowledge of his

139

self-betrayal. His mouth dropped, closed again.

'Now, wait a minute—'

'I don't understand,' Judy exclaimed. 'What did he do, Branch?'

Kindred was in no mood to spare her. 'He told Roth about my plan of moving Anchor stock across the Lease. When I got up there this morning I found an army of special deputies and a court order waiting to turn us back. At first I actually thought it was Gwen Marshall's doings.'

Judy's lips, pale against a colorless face, worked on words she couldn't utter.

'Oh!' she whispered at last. 'How could you?'

'It was the best thing for the ranch,' Hazen said. 'You'll realize it someday.'

'You betrayed us all!' she stormed at him. 'You wanted to be very sure we'd have to sell Anchor—at any price Roth cared to offer! It didn't matter what anyone else might want. It didn't even matter if you killed Gramps!' Her breast swelled and she swung her clenched fist blindly at his face.

Hazen, falling back a step, flung up a hand and caught the blow. He trapped her wrist, and Judy went wild.

'Stop it!' Earl said hoarsely . He had both her hands now and she twisted and kicked at him and tore at his grasp. Earl Hazen shook her savagely. 'By God you're my daughter and you're going to act like you knew it! Do you hear what I'm saying?'

'You're hurting me!'

Kindred had held himself in as long as he could. He shouted, 'Let go of her, Hazen!'

The words seemed to cut between them like the shearing edge of a knife. The struggling ceased.

'This is none of your business,' Earl Hazen said. 'Stay out of it, mister.'

'No! It makes no difference who you are. You have no right to maul her!'

Hazen had eased his grip slightly on Judy's arms and she seized the chance to break free. She stumbled away from her father and flung herself against Kindred, like a child turning to an adult for comforting. Sight of his daughter seeking this man's arms was too much for Hazen. He loosed a roar. His legs carried him forward and his fists swung at Kindred.

Hampered by the girl, Kindred could not ward off the first attack. Hazen's knuckles rasped across his face, drawing pain from the eye that was still discolored from his fight with Jay Benteen. Kindred flung up an arm and caught Hazen a blow on the chest that staggered him and made his leather heels squeal on the floorboards. But as soon as he regained balance Hazen rushed again, and Kindred had to put Judy aside and defend himself.

Hazen proved no fist fighter, no bunkhouse

141

brawler like Benteen. It was not hard to block his blows. Kindred brushed them aside, and then his own long-growing resentment toward his man took hold. He waded in on Hazen. The sound of striking blows and panting filled the room.

But the odds were too unfair, and the sight of Hazen's bloody, sweating face presently sobered Kindred. A kind of self-disgust shuddered through him. As Earl Hazen slammed back into the staircase railing, with a force that made it groan and nearly splinter, he held the next blow that would have followed up. His arm trembled with the effort to check it. He dropped both his hands and, standing there, shoulders hunched, head thrust forward, he said thickly, 'Let this go, Hazen! Don't make me kill you!'

Hazen crouched, staring at him through strings of blond hair that were plastered to his face by sweat. Blood and saliva hung in a thread from his slack lips. Barely able to stand, he dragged sobbing breath into his lungs and said with weak viciousness, 'I've told you once that you're fired. The court will back me up. Now, go on and get off this ranch—you cheap tough!'

'I'm going,' Kindred said. He heeled around and took two long strides toward the door.

'Wait,' Judy cried. 'I'm coming with you!'

Her father's voice was terrible with wrath: 'Judy!' But she caught up with Kindred and her hands clasped at his arm. 'I won't stay with him another minute!' she sobbed. 'You've got to take me!'

'You know I can't do that. Good-bye, Judy.'

He tried to free himself. Judy began to cry and tremble and cling to him all the harder.

'No, no! I mean it, Branch! I won't stay here!'

He sensed the nearness of hysteria. The death of the old man in the adjoining bedroom had brought Judy to the limit of what she could endure. She was speaking the literal truth—she couldn't stay alone here, with this father of hers. Knowing this, he only half heard the furious warning that Earl Hazen hurled at him: 'Be careful, Kindred! You do this, and you'll find yourself in trouble like you've never seen before!'

Forcing a comforting smile for Judy, Branch Kindred laid a hand upon her shoulder. 'All right,' he told her gently. 'Get whatever you need, and say good-bye to Sam. I'll take you in to Rock River. There, you'll be better able to think things over and know what you really want to do.'

*   *   *

To Frank Chaffee's esthetic eye, a herd of cattle had the clean, pure beauty of so many dollar marks on the hoof. His sense of beauty had been strongly roused and gratified by what

143

he had just seen grazing along the flats by the river, and this had put him in a fine mood.

'A little gaunt yet from the trail—I admit that,' he told Gwen Marshall, flicking the reins against the rumps of his buggy team. 'But Croyden Roth has good, sound stock there. Put them on decent grass and you'll see them start packing on the weight. Believe me,' he went on expansively, 'you'll make no mistake on this proposition! A wonderful out for you, my dear.'

Gwen maintained a moody silence. The banker knew his beef values, of course, but she couldn't keep her mind on the cattle they had been inspecting. Croyden Roth's crew interested her far more. Trail-herding cowboys were apt to be a fairly uncurried lot, especially at the end of a long drive, but these struck her as a bunch of toughsmen too familiar with the guns they wore on their hips and in their saddle boots. She couldn't see why Roth should have taken so large a crew to handle a mere thousand head. She understood that altogether some twenty riders had come in with the herd from New Mexico. Certainly a third that many would have been enough.

She peered from beneath the buggy top at the strong profile of this strange man riding alongside, a competent and powerful figure in the saddle. She recalled the warnings Branch Kindred had tried to give her concerning Croyden Roth, and at the thought of Branch, a keen stab of pain made her bite her lip and knot her fingers in her lap.

As the river road brought them into town, with the afternoon shadows lying like bars across the dust, Chaffee checked his team and leaned to speak across Gwen, including Roth in his question: 'What do you say? Shall we just go on to the bank now and arrange the terms? It won't take long to draw up the necessary papers.'

Scarcely knowing why she did it, Gwen heard herself protesting. 'That will take *some* time, won't it? It's so late. I really should get home and see if my little boy is all right. I left him with his grandfather.'

The banker made a slight face. It was as though he said, 'With Milt McCune? In that case, I don't blame you for worrying.' But, affably enough, he suggested, 'In the morning, perhaps?'

'I can't wait that long,' Roth objected. 'Those cattle of mine are trail-starved. They've already exhausted what graze was left on the flats. I'm going to have to start moving them up, first thing tomorrow.

'In that case,' the banker said, 'why don't the three of us get together in my office after supper? Then we can thrash the whole thing out to everyone's satisfaction. And meanwhile,' he added, smiling at Gwen, 'I can have a form ready for your signature, extending your loan.'

Gwen felt faint. She closed her eyes. The insistent pressure, the false air of friendliness with which this preposterous little man goaded and relentlessly pushed her, brought on a smothering sensation. But she knew her helplessness and she said, 'Very well,' in a muffled voice.

Chaffee cleared his throat, summoning up every ounce of persuasive charm as he beamed on the cattleman. 'And, Mr. Roth, we can see about opening an account for you. Right?'

'In good time,' Croyden Roth replied indifferently.

A moment later he touched his hatbrim to the woman and rode on—an erect, assured man, arrogant in his power and his expectations. Frank Chaffee drove Gwen around to her home, handed her down from the buggy without leaving his seat. 'This evening,' he said, showing her a toothy smile which she answered only with a nod. She left him and hurried into the house.

She closed the front door behind her. 'We're back here,' her father called from the kitchen. Gwen drew a deep breath, summoning strength that seemed constantly drained under the tensions of these days. She went along the hallway and halted in the kitchen door.

Milt McCune sat at the table with Billy in his lap, pine shavings scattered on the floor around him. He had been whittling a wooden sixgun of considerable exactness of detail. 'Well, son,' he said, 'here's your mother.' Billy gave a crow of delight, scrambled down and came hurrying to her. But Gwen scarcely noticed him. She saw Judy Hazen sitting across the table from Milt, and yonder, Branch Kindred leaning his hips against the edge of the sink, his arms folded, his grave eyes studying her face. It startled her beyond reason.

The little boy tugged at his mother's skirts, insisting that she see the gun. She bent and kissed him, murmuring, 'Yes, darling, it's very nice,' but her own words sounded dead to her. They sounded that way to Branch Kindred, too. She could tell by the expression on his bruised face.

She straightened as he told her, 'I'm sorry. If our being in your house distresses you, we had no business coming. We won't stay. I guess it was foolish to think that more talking could do any good.'

Gwen couldn't keep the coldness from her voice. 'Nothing has changed.'

'That's where you're wrong,' her father cut in. Milt McCune's big palms methodically folded the blades of his knife into the handle. 'There's been a passel of changes. For one thing, Sam Hazen is dead.'

She gasped. 'Dead!'

'Sometime in the night,' Kindred said.

Gwen turned to Judy. She recognized the

marks of deep grief, and pity stabbed her. 'I'm so terribly sorry!' she cried. 'What can I say?' She saw Judy's tremulous smile of thanks and a genuine protective impulse made her step forward and place a hand on Judy's shoulder.

'It's all right,' Judy said, a little shakily. 'I'm getting used to believing he's gone.'

'If there's anything in the world I can do—'

'Could you let her stay here with you?' Kindred asked.

Any jealousy Gwen might ever have felt vanished in the presence of this young girl's need. 'Why, of course. She should have another woman at a time like this. And there is none at Anchor.'

Billy was getting underfoot, with his eagerness for his mother's attention. Milt leaned and scooped him onto his lap. He said, 'I reckon that ain't precisely the point. Judy's left the ranch. Had a row with that no-good paw of hers, and walked out on him. Kindred, here, has gone and got himself fired.' His mouth twisted in wry humor at Gwen's shocked reaction. 'I told you things had been happening.'

'Gwen,' Kindred said, before she could find an answer, 'could I talk to you? Alone?'

She nodded and walked out of the kitchen and along the hall to the living room. She turned there, with her back to the round center table. Kindred came through the beaded archway and stopped before her. They

148

stood there gazing at each other, and it brought to mind other, happier occasions in the past. Branch settled his shoulders, and Gwen sensed that what he had to say took an effort.

'You're wondering how I had the nerve to come here,' he said. 'You're wondering how I could force Judy and myself on you, after what happened yesterday in the store. Well, maybe now you see the answer. I'm through at Anchor, so you've got no reason to include the ranch in your feelings against me. I'm hoping that may make a difference, Gwen.'

He paused, and when the silence endured too long, Gwen said from a dry throat, 'Go on.'

'This morning,' he said, 'I tried to take some beef across the Lease—as I told you I was going to—and put them on the higher meadows where they'd at least have a chance. At the boundary the sheriff and a bunch of Roth's gunmen stopped me. They were all wearing deputy's badges. Johnson had a court order forbidding us to cross the Lease. We had to turn back, Gwen. And there's no telling, now, what will happen to the cattle and the ranch itself.'

'Branch,' she said. 'Branch, I didn't know a thing about this. I swear I didn't.'

'I know. I admit I thought at first you might have. I thought you'd tipped my hand to Roth, and I'm damned glad it wasn't so. Because— Gwen, I'm wondering if there's any chance—

149

now that I'm not involved any more, now that I'm probably going to be leaving this range for good—if—there's any chance you could reconsider? For Judy's sake, Gwen. And for the men who used to work for me, men who are loyal to their iron. Is there any way to keep you from going ahead with your dealings with Croyden Roth?' He seemed to gather himself, there, cold and hard and accusing. 'Is money *really* this important to you?'

'Damn it!' Milt McCune cut in, and they both whirled toward the doorway. He had followed them from the kitchen, uninvited. He had stood in the archway, listening to their talk, and now he was glowering at Kindred with brown eyes gone dark and indignant. 'What are you sayin' to her, Kindred? When are you goin' to get it through your head that it ain't Gwen's wanting—it's the bank!'

'The bank?' Branch Kindred showed them a blank and baffled expression. 'I don't understand, Milt.'

'Frank Chaffee holds a lien against the store,' Milt said. 'A big one. He's been holding it over her head like a club. Chaffee's playing Roth's game, from the day that bastard showed up here. Either Gwen delivers the Dumont Section, Branch, or the bank calls in its loan. For Billy's sake, she's had to go along!'

Blood drained out of Kindred's face, leaving its swollen bruises all the more livid. 'Gwen,'

150

he said hoarsely, 'why didn't you tell me all this?'

'You never gave me much of a chance, Branch.'

'And to think that I—' He looked down at his right hand, the hand he had laid across her cheek in that terrible quarrel at the store. His mouth twisted. He formed the hand into a tight fist and slammed it hard upon the table. 'What can I say?' he groaned. 'How can I apologize?'

He reached for Gwen, but the tension was suddenly too much for her. She turned on trembling legs and fled, afraid of what her tortured nerves might do if she stayed. As she rushed blindly from the room Branch Kindred spoke her name and tried to follow, but Milt McCune dropped a heavy hand upon his shoulder.

'You better leave her go,' Milt said. 'You don't know what that girl's been goin' through since Bill died. And no help from anybody. Least of all me, I guess,' he added in bitter self-disgust.

'Besides,' he went on as the younger man showed indecision, 'talkin' will do no good just now. Talkin' won't change anything—like gettin' rid of that note at the bank, or makin' it possible for her to do anything but go through with the deal with Roth.'

Slowly, Kindred let stiffness go out of his body.

'When she's ready to listen to any apology, I'll try to think of the words,' he said. 'Right now I'd better leave. I'll take Judy with me.'

'No need of that. She's welcome to stay. It would do both of them good.'

But Kindred shook his head. 'Having her here could make trouble for Gwen, with Roth and Chaffee—and her own conscience. God knows she's under enough pressure. Judy will be perfectly all right at the hotel, Milt. I'll take her there.'

McCune saw the sense of the argument. 'You could be right, Branch. I'll tell Gwen. If I can, I'll put in a word for you—not that she's apt to listen to much I got to say. Or, that I can rightly blame her either! Reckon I've never done nothin' but let that girl down. It ain't a pleasant thing to know about yourself, Kindred.'

*   *   *

They had left Judy's little suitcase at the hotel. Kindred got it from the clerk, and the key to a room, and escorted her up the creaking staircase and along the dingy hall. Judy, very subdued and quiet, waited without speaking while he unlocked the door and let her in, and placed the suitcase by the bed. He opened the window and put fresh air to work at the room's mustiness. Looking around with distaste, he said, 'It could be worse. Try to get some rest.

I'll come back later and we can have some dinner downstairs. You'll be all right here.'

'All right,' she said. 'And thanks—so very much.'

He smiled, squeezing her hand, but when he turned to go she said, 'No, Branch. Wait.' She stepped past him and closed the door and stood with her hand on the knob.

'Branch, what will you do?'

'I don't know, Judy,' he said, speaking the solemn truth. 'Frankly, I don't. After today I feel like a man who's had all the props knocked out from under him—and doesn't know where to look for more.'

She shook her head a little. 'It's the first time I've ever known you to be unsure of yourself, or the road you meant to travel.'

'Disappointed?' He smiled. 'Sorry, Judy. I'm really no more than human.'

She said, fiercely, 'I could never be disappointed in you!' but then she faltered. 'About—Gwen Marshall,' she murmured, and he could see the effort it took for her to utter the name. 'You still think the world of her, don't you, Branch?'

There was only one answer. He nodded.

Judy swallowed something in her throat. 'She's a very fine person,' she said, gallantly. 'And the little boy is a darling. I'm sure you can—work things out.'

Her eyes were bright with love and sacrifice, and Kindred felt very humble before her.

Could he give no girl anything but pain? He took a long breath. 'Judy,' he began. And then came the tramp of boots in the hall, and the sudden pounding of a fist on the door.

Judy jerked her hand from the knob. Kindred challenged sharply: 'Who's there?'

Somebody jerked the door open. Kindred caught the glint of a drawn gun. He made an involuntary movement toward his holster but checked it. The weapon's muzzle leveled on him, and above it he saw Cliff Johnson's face—scowling, beardstubbled, still showing the stains of the long ride he'd made down from the Dumont Lease.

'It's the law, Kindred,' the sheriff said. 'Second time today I've had to tangle with you. Looks to me like you're trying to set a record. Now, keep your hand away from that holster and don't make trouble.'

'What's chewing you this time?' Kindred demanded in cold contempt. And then he caught sight of Ed Farrar and Earl Hazen waiting out in the hall, and a chilly premonition came to him.

Haven shoved into the room. He looked at Kindred, and he looked at Judy, and a grin of pure malevolence twisted his fist-lumpy mouth.

'You've figured it already, Kindred. Abducting a minor is a serious charge in this state, my tough friend.'

Kindred felt Judy recoil against him, heard

154

her gasp of horror. He said, 'You'll never make this stick, Hazen. Don't humiliate Judy by trying it.'

'I know what I'm doing!' Plainly there was no reasoning with the man, no getting past the resentments that were pushing him. 'We'll see what Judge Gore has to say about it. You, Judy—get your things. You're coming home with me!'

'Never! I won't—'

'You're still my daughter and you're still under age. You'll do whatever I say, girl. Farrar, get her suitcase.'

Ed Farrar hung back. His eyes sought Kindred's in acute misery. But an order was an order, and with an unhappy shrug he slid into the room and picked up the bag Kindred had set beside the bed. He held it awkwardly, swallowing, Adam's apple bobbing, waiting.

The sheriff's gun and full attention stayed on Kindred. 'And this gent, Mr. Hazen? What do you want done with him?'

'I want him jailed. He thinks he can get away with anything. Maybe a cell will tame him down a little.'

'No!' Judy burst out, unable to contain herself. 'No! You can't do this!' She clutched Kindred's arm desperately. 'Not to Branch! My leaving Anchor wasn't any way his fault. Do what you like with me but—'

His weak face set and stern, Earl Hazen seized his daughter, dragging her roughly away

155

from Kindred. Judy tried to break free, and couldn't, and then she surrendered, crying openly like a child. And when Kindred started a move to her aid, the sheriff's gun was there, its black muzzle almost touching his belt buckle, its hammer pronging back under Cliff Johnson's thumb.

'All right, mister,' the sheriff said. 'You heard what her father said. It's good enough for me. Anything you got to say about being alone in a hotel room with a girl as young as this one, you can save for Judge Gore—and you better make it sound convincing! Right now I'll take that gun.'

Slowly, Kindred passed it over.

CHAPTER TEN

The cell was a moldy, cement-floored room, about six feet square, with no other furnishings than the strap-iron bed chained to the wall and the slop jar underneath. There were three good paces from the barred window to the barred door, and Kindred traveled that course futilely through the slow hours. Finally he lay on the hard bunk and brooded over the tangled mess he had succeeded in making of things. He must have dozed off, presently, because the rasp of a key in the lock jerked him up and he found that the day had died and

156

dusk was in the cell with him. A wall lamp just outside laid yellow light and barred shadows on him, as well as the shadows of the men clustered outside the door.

Kindred pushed himself to a sitting position as the door swung open. The three who tramped into the cell were Jay Benteen, Bart Hooker, and a third man whom he remembered seeing at the Lease that morning. Three big men, all with deputy's badges on their chests. In the corridor the jailer, a helpless oldster with a gimp leg and a perpetual wheezing cough, jangled his keyring and fidgeted uneasily.

The newcomers filled the tiny space. Benteen loomed over the bunk with legs spread wide and craggy fists planted on his hips, above the sag of the filled gunbelt. Lamplight gleamed on the wiry red hair that covered his hard skull.

'Take a look, boys!' he said, with heavy amusement. 'This is what finally come of the ruckus he raised with me the other day over the Hazen filly. Turns out he just wanted that young stuff for himself!'

Benteen's coarse laughter bounced off the narrow walls. His breath carried its freight of whisky but the man was sober—cold sober, and savoring a coming pleasure. Kindred knew with a sure fatality what was ahead of him, but he could not let the man have his way unchallenged. He came to his feet. He said in

157

a leaden voice, 'You can keep your cheap talk away from Judy Hazen.'

'Yeah?' White teeth glinted as the trail boss grinned. A lifting of his chest telegraphed the first blow, before his fist started its arc.

Kindred stepped away from the swing, but the bunk and the stone wall crowded him. Benteen's fist caught him on a hunched shoulder. He threw an answering punch and felt it bounce off the side of Benteen's skull, aware even as he heard Benteen's grunt of pain that he was just baiting an angry bear. This time he had no chance and he knew it.

Benteen snapped an order and his two companions moved in on Kindred. He tried to ward them off but they came from opposite directions. They blocked the punches he threw, and they grabbed his arms and clamped them down in such a fashion that he could not break free. Helpless, he braced himself as Benteen very slowly and deliberately formed a fist and cocked it, ready to drive it squarely into the middle of the prisoner's face.

'Don't mark him up too much,' Croyden Roth said.

'All right,' Benteen said agreeably, and lowered his arm a few inches. Kindred had a glimpse of Roth watching from beyond the barred door, one of his expensive cigars burning between his lips. The jailer had vanished, leaving Kindred alone with these enemies.

And then the ready fist came sledging home, into the middle of Kindred's body. He had sucked in breath, firmed his hard belly muscles against the blow, but it tore right through and agony was a hard, burning knot in him. He doubled under it, his weight pulling on his imprisoned arms. Still, his legs were free, and he managed to bring a boot up. He heard Benteen's howl of surprise and pain as its sharp toe dug into the heavy muscle of his thigh.

'A tough rooster,' Croyden Roth commented. 'Maybe too tough, for the three of you.' He chuckled, a soft ripple of malicious mirth, and he was still laughing as he turned and strolled from the jail building at an unconcerned and leisurely pace, leaving the aroma of his cigar behind him.

Roth's amusement was a goad that dug sharply into his trail boss. An indrawn breath flared Benteen's flattened nostrils. 'Hold him, damn you!' he snarled at his helpers, and moved in on Kindred.

That initial belly blow had done its work. Drained of strength, all but paralyzed, Kindred could do nothing now to defend himself. His efforts to tear free from the hands that gripped him availed nothing. Brutally and methodically Benteen went about his task, and the fists that sledged into his victim became the rhythmic, slamming pistoning of some kind of machine. The blows smashed against Kindred's heart, his ribs, his empty stomach. His arms seemed

159

about to wrench from their sockets with the sagging weight as his knees weakened.

He felt sure that his ribs were splintered and his internal organs torn loose. Breath left his body. A huge, burning nausea filled him. Then, through a red haze of pain, hard knuckles slammed full against his jaw and despite the hands that held him he went down.

'Pick him up,' Benteen's voice panted from a far distance.

The hands tugged and lifted, but Kindred's legs had dissolved and his limp weight was too much for the pair of them to hold up so Benteen could continue working on him. He heard the big man's curse. Dimly he caught the sound of metal sliding against leather, and through glazed eyes he saw two Benteens and two six-guns lifting, their barrels twin shimmerings of reflected lamplight. He waited for the descent of the steel against his skull that would end this torment and let him drop all the way into oblivion.

It never came. Instead, there was Cliff Johnson's voice, demanding in a tone of shocked horror, 'What's going on here, anyway?' And suddenly everything stopped.

'This is none of your damn—' Jay Benteen began, but Bart Hooker cut in on him, with a warning murmur: 'Easy!' The hands released Kindred. He tried hard to stand but the iron edge of the bunk struck the backs of his legs and he collapsed upon it, gasping. He didn't lose consciousness. The gleam of the corridor lamp splintered, darkened momentarily. Then things took on solid shape.

He heard Cliff Johnson say, in a tone of unusual firmness, 'I think the three of you had better get out of here while we see just what you've done to him!'

They didn't like this order. There was some grumbling, but another word from Hooker ended it and they went tramping out of the cell. Kindred fought wind back into his lungs. He tried to pull himself up to a sitting position. Hands supported him. He looked around in surprise to see Earl Hazen regarding him with an expression of sober concern.

'If we hadn't got here when we did,' Hazen said, 'they could have killed him. I never wanted anything like that. You understand, don't you, Sheriff?'

'Well, they weren't following orders from me!' Johnson answered shortly.

Both of them working at guilty consciences, Kindred thought dully. They've got to clear themselves, first of all. But it didn't matter much. How bad was he hurt? That was all that mattered.

The old turnkey showed up with a bottle. Johnson uncorked it.

'Take a couple good swallows of this,' he ordered, and put it to Kindred's lips. The strong, raw whisky ran into his throat, down his gullet. It met the churning nausea in his

161

empty belly and came up again. He bent and poured it out on the concrete. The sheriff jumped back.

'See if you can find the doctor,' Johnson ordered.

'I don't think he's in town, just now,' the jailer said, but he hobbled out.

Shuddering with churning emptiness and the burn of his raw throat, Kindred flapped his hand at them. 'If you really want to do something for me,' he gasped, 'get the hell away!' Oddly enough, he felt better already, his head clearing. This made him begin to doubt that he was seriously hurt. Benteen had been interrupted too soon. He felt sore deep down, where the heavy fists had landed, but he couldn't detect the stab of any broken rib, or of other disruption of his vitals.

Then what Johnson was saying broke through, and he lifted his head to stare uncomprehendingly from one man to the other.

'We're here to free you, Kindred.'

'It's Judy,' Earl Hazen explained heavily. 'She's been pleading with me ever since you were arrested. She—well, she finally promised to come home with me and stop making trouble if I'd drop charges. I've agreed—on one condition, naturally.'

'And that is?'

'You're to leave this range for good. At once!'

Leaving Anchor to you and Croyden Roth, Kindred thought. He ran an unsteady palm across his face, feeling the cold sweat that beaded his skin. Rebellion ran strong in him but it died under the inexorable weight of realities. He had no real choice. He had fought hard for Sam and for Judy and—by circumstances—for Earl Hazen, and he had lost every round. Roth had countered each move. The last real hope had ended when he learned the truth about the economic chains that bound Gwen Marshall to Roth's will.

He couldn't do any more. He couldn't defy the legal club that Hazen poised over him. But he hesitated so long that Earl Hazen grew impatient. 'Well, what about it?' Hazen demanded. 'Do you take my terms or do you want to rot in that cell?'

'Your horse is saddled and waiting,' Cliff Johnson added. 'Believe me, if you're smart you'll take this chance. I can tell you now that Judge Gore will throw the book at you.'

There was no doubting his sincerity. Kindred dragged air into tortured lungs. 'All right. Let me see if I can get on my feet.'

They had to help him, but once he got off the bunk he waved them away. He stood there steadying himself, a palm against the rough stone wall. Dizziness and nausea threatened to engulf him again, but this passed and his legs took on strength. His stomach muscles, punished by Benteen's pile-driver fists, felt so

163

sore that he thought he might break at the middle, but this seemed the worst of his real injuries. He walked out of the cell, staggering, lurching into the door frame with a force that nearly threw him.

He was moving steadily enough, however, as he let them usher him down the short corridor and into the sheriff's office. There, in a chair tilted back against the big county map that hung on the wall, Jay Benteen sat calmly smoking. The gun in Benteen's holster jutted from his hip. The deputy's badge shone on his thick chest. Hooker and the third Roth man were not in evidence.

No one said anything. Johnson plumped down behind his desk and fetched up a manila envelope containing the prisoner's personal effects. Kindred signed the receipt, put his money and watch in his pockets. He threaded his belt through the loops and pulled it tight.

'My gun,' he said. 'Don't I get my gun?'

Earl Hazen began a motion of protest but checked it. Sheriff Johnson seemed to hesitate, then pushed back his chair. The cartridge belt and filled holster hung from a nail-studded board in the corner beyond Jay Benteen's chair. Johnson was on his feet when Benteen spoke.

'No gun,' Benteen said.

'This is still my office,' Cliff Johnson said. 'I'll continue to run it!'

With no expression at all, with nothing more

164

than a meager shake of his bullet-shaped, red-thatched skull, Benteen repeated, 'I said no gun.' And his hand came to rest on the butt of the revolver jutting from his own holster.

Johnson looked at the hand. He opened his mouth, closed it again and pushed the tip of his tongue through to swipe across his lower lip.

'You going to turn me out empty-handed,' Kindred said, 'for Roth's men to murder at their own convenience?'

His words stung a flush from the sheriff but otherwise they did no good. Cliff Johnson had gone too far to back away now. He was fundamentally a decent man, but he'd given over his own will to the dominance of the political higher-ups who kept him in his job. He saw himself well enough, then. He saw his integrity last and his office taken over by thugs he had been persuaded to deputize—and he saw his own complete helplessness.

This realization shaped itself in the sheriff's scared eyes. The defiance died, and Kindred understood that he was looking at a broken man. He heard the breath run out of Earl Hazen—a slow, ragged sigh which said that even he could sense what was happening here.

'Get going,' Benteen said softly.

Kindred walked out into the early dusk.

The street was nearly deserted. The crowd of loafers around the stage station at its end had long since dispersed. Smoke from supper

165

fires rose from house chimneys into the hard steel sky. Down in the dusky strip between the buildings, a few horses stood tied and a shadowy figure or two showed on the hard-beaten paths. Light from the open door showed Kindred the mount—his own stockinged roan—tied before the jail. His saddle and possible sack were in place everything ready, just as the sheriff had said. All he had to do was mount and ride.

He walked out to the horse. He jerked loose the knot that held the reins, and a sound at his back made him turn. Benteen had followed him out of the jail. Benteen had stopped just beside the door, to lean his shoulders against the stone and wait and watch Kindred's departure. Kindred found the stirrup on the second try, he hauled himself up, his arms shaky with the effort it took to lift his weight into the saddle.

And then he froze.

From beneath the overhang fronting a store directly across from him, two men had stepped into the street. There was still light enough to identify Bart Hooker. Panic touched Kindred. Mentally he rummaged through the contents of the warbag lashed behind his saddle, trying to remember anything at all that could serve as a weapon. He weighed his chances of kicking his roan into a run, escaping in one unexpected burst of flight. Those two facing him, and Benteen at his back, could dump him before he covered a dozen yards. Yet he was poised, tense to make the try, when he saw the real intent of Hooker and his partner.

They were mounting up, going about it with a clear singleness of purpose. Watching them swing into their saddles, he knew they had been waiting for him. They sat their horses, and Hooker's voice reached out over the acrid dust.

'All right, friend. Move on like the sheriff said. We'll be following along. We'll be your escort, just to make sure you really do get out of town.'

'How far out?' Kindred said. 'How far will I get?'

Bart Hooker seemed to think that remark was funny. He chuckled, enjoying it.

'Ride and see,' he said.

Under the arcade which these two had left a moment ago, a single red eye of light rose in an arc as someone raised a glowing cigar to his mouth. Kindred made out the shape of the man, leaning easily against a roof prop. He saw the cigar flare and glow, revealing Croyden Roth's face as the man sucked smoke from the burning weed. And a hard, hopeless impulse sent him over there.

He walked his horse across the street, straight between the mounts of that other pair who drew back with a hard alertness as he came. When he halted they were on either side of him, bracketing him in what could be a fatal whipsaw. But he didn't think about that.

167

Instead, he laid his stare directly on the dim figure under the roof.

'All right,' he said. 'It looks like you win. But don't be too damned sure, Roth. These things have a way of working out. You might climb a little high one of these days—and someone might have to pull you down.'

Roth puffed at his smoke. His face, in the red glow, was utterly calm, smugly complacent. 'At least,' he said, 'we both know it won't be you. Don't we, Kindred?'

'Might be,' Kindred said. 'Might not. These big guns of yours may kill me, but do you really know they will? And if they don't—if there is anything more—well, you may be hearing from me.' His voice lowered, without his willing it. 'Out of the dark, maybe, some night. Look out for the hands you can't see, Roth. And listen for footsteps you can't hear behind you. Because—that'll be me!'

Oddly, Croyden Roth didn't answer. But he was still standing there when Kindred pulled his horse around and started up the street.

Kindred's executioners fell in behind.

CHAPTER ELEVEN

Earl Hazen traveled the faded hotel carpeting to the door of his daughter's room, but with his hand lifted to knock he found himself

168

hesitating, his mouth pulled down in a fretful scowl of uneasiness. Settling his shoulders, he laid his knuckles firmly against the wood and said, in a voice that he roughened to hide the irresolution that filled him: 'Judy? It's your father. I want you to come down to supper.'

Her words came back, completely cold, and sounding oddly muffled. 'No, thanks. I'm not hungry.'

'Now, I know that isn't true. I'm starved, and I'm sure you must be.'

'I tell you, I couldn't eat anything.'

'And I'm telling you you're going to stop this nonsense! We made a bargain, you and I, and I've kept my part of it.'

There was a long silence behind the door. Finally the girl said, 'All right.'

'That's better. I'll give you five minutes. I'll be waiting down in the lobby.' He meant to leave, then, but something held him there still. He spoke again and the stiffening had gone out of his voice; it must, he thought, reveal every bit of the anguish that tortured him. 'Judy? Are you listening to me, girl?'

'Yes.'

'I want you to know that I really mean what I say. I hope were going to be able to start over now, you and I. To forget the past, and get off to a better beginning together. After all, you are my daughter.'

No answer at all, for a moment.

'I'll be down,' she said, 'in five minutes.'

He had to be satisfied with that.

When she came down stairs, she showed the strain of what she had been through that day. Hazen felt a pang of guilt which was replaced by a stirring resentment at her behavior. He tossed aside the week-old newspaper that he had been pretending to read, and rose and walked across the lobby to meet her. With no expression at all, she let him escort her into the dingy dining room, and her arm was cold to his touch.

The meal itself turned out to be a total failure, and only partly because of the indigestible food. Judy wouldn't talk to him, would give him almost no response in spite of every effort. He had always held himself to be a man not entirely devoid of charm, but with this daughter of his he had no success at all. Too great a wall stood between them, and her unyielding silence built it higher with every uncomfortable moment they spent together. Why, he found himself wondering in exasperation, did it matter so much to him? What difference could her cold disdain make? Was it her resemblance to her mother—the girl he had loved, so many years ago, and whose tragic death had seemed to snap all the tenuous mooring of his reckless nature? Or was there only guilt, a hidden sense of shame, aroused by her hatred?

Suddenly throwing down his fork he reached across the table and clutched her

170

hand. It lay yielding and limp beneath his own. '*Please*, Judy,' he said, frankly begging. 'Give me this one chance, won't you? If you only will, you'll see that we can have good times together. I'll get you out of this.' He indicated the drab dining room, with a nod that took in the hotel, the town, the range stretching into the night. 'We can go to Denver, San Francisco—anywhere you like. We'll see things you never dreamed of in this forgotten backwash. We'll make a lady of you.'

Her eyes lifted to his, almost the first time she had looked at him during the meal. 'Maybe,' she said, 'I don't want to be a lady. Maybe I don't want anything except what I've always had—the things that you want to take away from me!'

'I see.' He withdrew his hand, a cold weight settling finally and solidly within him. 'You've made up your mind, then. *Whatever* I do, you're going to go on resenting me.'

'How can I help it?' she said. 'You forced a promise from me. I'll keep it. But beyond that, please don't expect me to go.'

Earl Hazen stood up, tossing his napkin down beside his plate. 'Finish your meal,' he said shortly. 'I'll locate Ed Farrar and have him take you home.'

Farrar was in the hotel barroom, draped over the counter with a shot glass of whisky in front of him. He took his orders in surly silence, downed his drink and walked away, leaving Earl Hazen furious.

The very ranch hands treated him with ill-concealed contempt. He had seen it in their eyes, when they rode down from the hills to find old Sam dead and Branch Kindred fired, and Judy fled with him to town. He had heard grumblings among them, and for a moment he'd had the feeling that they were going to quit him. That they hadn't was, he suspected, due to the influence of this same Ed Farrar, the oldest, or nearly the oldest hand. But it was loyalty to a brand, and no personal liking for their new boss, that held them on. Ed Farrar's manner just now proved it.

In an increasingly poor mood, he caught the bartender's eye and had a bottle and glass set before him. He poured his drink. The bar mirror showed him the halfdoors leading to the lobby. About to lift his glass, he paused as he saw, in reflection, the three men who had entered the lobby and were standing at the foot of the stairs—Croyden Roth, Jay Benteen, and another of Roth's men. They conversed briefly, intently. Two of them hurried out of the lobby, while Roth started to climb the steps. But then, with hand on railing, Roth paused. Next, he swung away and came toward the bar, frowning and absorbed. As he pushed open the swinging connecting door, Hazen swung around to greet him. 'Will you join me?' he asked.

Roth swiveled his head sharply, as if Hazen

172

had interrupted some engrossing thoughts. Except for the bartender, they were alone in the room. Roth nodded shortly to the invitation, said, 'Thanks,' and took his place as Hazen signaled for another glass and filled it.

Hazen watched Roth down his whisky, holding his own untasted in his hand. He said, 'I suppose you heard about my father?'

'What? Oh, yes, I did. Too bad.'

'It was very sudden. But he was an old man, and I'm given to understand now that he'd been having trouble with his heart. Nobody bothered to tell me while he was alive. It was very like that fellow Kindred, to know about it and keep me in the dark.' He drank and put down his glass. 'Well, we're rid of Kindred anyway. Have another?'

He started to take the bottle again, but Roth shook his head. 'No thanks.' Roth reached into a pocket and brought out his cigar case and extracted a weed, but this time he failed to offer one to Hazen. He seemed more than half unaware of Hazen's presence, held in that curious absorption. But Earl Hazen's own purposes were set now and he proceeded doggedly with what he had to say.

'I was thinking we might get together, whenever you find convenient. Discuss some business.'

'Business?'

'Why, yes. As soon as the change of ownership clears the courts, there's really no

173

reason we shouldn't be able to go ahead with the deal we talked about in Kansas City. In fact, I'm quite anxious to get the ranch sold and be quit of this God-forsaken country.'

Roth seemed to be considering this as he bit off the end of his cigar, brought out a match and deliberately snapped it alight. Hazen watched him cup the flame with his palms, and puff the smoke to life. Now, he thought. *Now*, damn it.

'Sorry,' Roth said curtly and dropped the blackened match into the bar spittoon. 'I'm afraid I'm not interested.'

'Not interested!' Hazen almost reeled.

'Your hearing is good,' Roth said indifferently, and walked out of the building.

At first, Earl Hazen couldn't move. Then he plunged after Roth. He caught the cattleman on the porch outside. He grabbed the man's arm and forcibly pulled him around. Light from an oil lamp burning over the hotel entrance fell across Roth's heavy face. He looked coolly annoyed.

'See here!' Hazen stammered. 'I—well, after all, don't I deserve an explanation?'

Croyden Roth freed his arm, 'There's nothing to explain, I'm simply not in the market for your ranch, Mr. Hazen. Without the Dumont Section, it seems to me you have very little to sell.'

'But Anchor is still a valuable property. I'll make you a good price.'

'For a ranch without any summer range?' Croyden Roth said. 'I'm willing to wait. Let's see how much the place is worth to you six months from now.'

A cold fist squeezed itself tight in Hazen's middle. He felt the thudding of his pulse, the constricted passage of his shallow breathing. 'Damn you!' The words started as a shout but they passed his trembling lips as little more than a strangled whisper. 'Then is this the pay I get for bringing you to this country, for giving you the warning that kept Branch Kindred from crossing the Lease this morning? For putting Kindred out of your way for good? I've been the same as a traitor, all because I listened to you! By God, I ought to—'

'Yes?' Roth snapped. 'You'll do what?' He waited, and in the silence that followed his lips curled scornfully. 'You won't do anything, Hazen. You're a coward and a fool. Eventually I'll want what's left of that ranch of yours, and when I do I won't have to buy it. I'll take it. And you'll do nothing then, either!'

He walked down the wide steps, and Earl Hazen let him go. In that moment he knew, at last, what he was and what he had done.

It was a cruel knowledge.

*   *   *

Croyden Roth strolled toward the bank through early evening stillness, a man fairly

175

well pleased with himself and with his projects. He had enjoyed his scene with Hazen. There was pleasure in knocking the props from under a fool, cutting him down to his true littleness. It added to a man's own stature, and in this case it had broken and settled a mood that had lain heavy on Roth during the past hour—in fact, since Branch Kindred rode out of town with Roth's killers behind him.

Roth didn't know why, but his last interview with Kindred had left him unsatisfied, unsettled. In some odd way, Kindred had bested him in that exchange. Grudgingly Roth had to admit that the man had strength. He was no mere tough, no heavy-fisted cow-country jay who'd managed somehow to draw down a foreman's wages. Kindred was a real man, with keen intelligence and the courage to face certain death. Indeed, Croyden Roth had felt a gnawing, unsettling suspicion that Branch Kindred might be a better man than himself, and this he could not accept. It had angered and corroded him, until—through taking it out on Hazen—he had managed to regain his self-esteem.

Now, with Sam Hazen dead and Branch Kindred out of the way, he had good cause for confidence. He had trod a tight line since he came here, with hands empty and his New Mexican adventure collapsed behind him. He had had to juggle, play man against man—a pursuit at which he excelled. He had faced moments when the hand he held was shaky, when the faintest bluff by his opponents could have exposed the weakness of a four-card flush. Yet he had bluffed them all, and now the game was turning in his favor. His strategy had justified itself.

Kindred had been the greatest problem, but that fool Earl Hazen had done him the favor of removing Kindred and Bart Hooker would finish the job. He could count on Hooker for that. Hooker had proved himself a good man—as dangerous with a gun as Jay Benteen, and possessed of a razor-keen intellect that was much more valuable than Benteen's brute power. Jay would get himself killed one of these days, thanks to his bullheaded lack of foresight, but in Hooker, he would have a new second-in-command available when the need came.

So Roth walked up the steps of the bank, toward the meeting with Chaffee and Gwen Marshall which would put the final touches to all his planning.

The shades were drawn and the main room of the bank appeared dark. But at his knock, footsteps sounded and Frank Chaffee himself opened the door. A long streak of light spilled across the dark room from the door of the banker's private office. 'Am I early?' Roth asked pleasantly.

'No,' Chaffee said, and from the very tone of the man's voice Roth drew a warning

'There's a hitch.'

'What do you mean? What sort of a hitch?'

Chaffee didn't answer. He turned the key in the lock. Roth followed him across the big room, traveling up that path of lamplight to the half-opened office door. Entering, Roth saw Gwen Marshall, white and tense, sitting in a chair beside the desk. He was surprised to see Judge Henry Gore—a dried-up, cantankerous man who resembled a goat, even to the straggling whiskers. A shrewd man, the Judge. Nobody liked him but he held reins of power in his dry, yellow-skinned hands. He regarded Roth with hooded black eyes set in an impassive yellow mask of a face.

Frank Chaffee was flushed with anger. The banker walked with ruffled dignity to drop into his padded swivel chair, and laid plump, hairless hands upon the desk's neat top. He seemed to be holding himself in with great effort.

'Mrs. Marshall,' he said, 'tells me she has changed her mind about the Dumont Section.'

'Oh?' Roth got a grip on himself. 'In what way?'

'I've decided I can't accept your proposition,' she said.

'But you've already accepted.'

'I haven't signed anything.'

'You made a verbal agreement,' Roth said. 'Frank Chaffee is my witness to that.'

The banker nodded.

'He only heard me agree that I'd come here tonight,' Gwen Marshall said. 'Well, I have. And now I'm telling you that I've changed my mind.'

Roth studied her for a long while, and he had the brown taste on the back of his tongue that often came when he encountered serious trouble. Anger surged in him, but he must control it. He could feel Judge Gore's cold scrutiny. It touched him like a clammy, physical contact. Play it out, he told himself. Play your hand, man.

'It isn't quite this simple,' he said briskly. 'Not for me. I took your promise at its face value. I've gone ahead and made my plans—'

'Yes,' Gwen Marshall said, and he caught the tight irony in her voice. 'I have a pretty good idea of the nature of those plans.'

Frank Chaffee shifted in his chair. 'You're talking riddles.'

'Am I?'

'Someone,' Roth said, 'has obviously been pumping you full of lies about me and my motives. I wonder who it could have been? Our friend Kindred?'

'What he told me wasn't lies, Mr. Roth!'

'My dear woman!' the banker exclaimed. 'Don't you know Branch Kindred is in jail?'

'I know it.'

'And you know why, I suppose?' Roth asked, letting scorn touch his firm, clean-shaven mouth. 'He took Earl Hazen's minor daughter

179

away from the ranch, against her father's wishes, and was later found alone with her in a room at the hotel. *That's* the man who's been trying to poison people's minds against me.'

'It's not the way you and the sheriff and Earl Hazen try to make it out! He's not that kind of man!'

'I see. I think things are beginning to come clear, now, about this decision you say you've made. You're really quite transparent, Mrs. Marshall. You have some idea, perhaps, that you can trade with Hazen by letting him have the lease, and buy Kindred's way out of the mess he's got himself in. Well,' he added, knowing from her reaction that he had guessed truly, 'it so happens that Kindred has already been freed—and has left the country. He quit town an hour ago. You've seen the last of him.'

Slowly she came to her feet, a hand on the desk as though she needed to steady herself. 'I don't believe you!'

The Judge spoke then, for the first time. He wagged his whiskered head and said, 'It's true enough, though it was done without my knowledge. Earl Hazen made terms and the man had sense enough to know they were the best he would get.'

'You see?' Roth persisted, cruelly. 'Your precious Kindred has saved his own skin. You'll never see him again on this range. And there's the reward for your loyalty.'

'Under the circumstances,' the Judge

180

suggested, 'are you sure you wouldn't like to reconsider the whole thing?'

Her breast lifted under the stress of cramped breathing. She swallowed, with apparent difficulty. 'No,' she said in a hoarse, painful whisper. 'It isn't true.'

Frank Chaffee's plump palm plopped loudly on the desktop. 'This is enough to make any man lose patience!' He rattled a drawer open and took a paper from it and laid the paper in front of the woman. 'This is the renewal of your note,' he said. 'I went to the trouble of having it drawn. All it needs is your signature. Would you prefer that I tear it up?'

The pressures were building in the woman, visibly. She stared at the paper, plainly seeing the import of her answer, unable to frame it. But as Roth searched her face, pale and strained and harried though it was, he sensed that she couldn't be intimidated.

'Am I allowed to ask,' he said harshly, 'what you intend to do with the property? Lease it again to your precious friend Earl Hazen?'

He waited, and she let him wait.

'Maybe,' she said. 'But with a cancellation clause in the event that he sells Anchor.'

She let that sink in, and her defiant eyes challenged all of them.

'I hope I make myself clear, gentlemen. It's not Anchor I'm concerned about. It's not Hazen—or even Branch Kindred. It's a whole range. I look around me and I see what you've done to it, Mr. Roth. I see your gunmen walking the streets wearing deputy's badges, and the Judge and the sheriff and Frank Chaffee eating out of your hand. I think of the things Branch tried to tell me—and even though I wouldn't listen, even though you've managed to break him and run him out of the country—I know now that what he said was true. The Lease can lie empty before I'll let it fall into your hands.'

'Are you finished?' Roth said icily.

'Not quite. Until I woke up to the truth,' she admitted, in bitter self-condemnation, 'I was a coward, bound by the fear of losing what security I had. Well, I've stopped being afraid. Of you Mr. Roth—and of *you*, Frank Chaffee!' She whirled on the banker, lips curling with contempt. 'You're a very little man, Frank. Go ahead—take the store, my husband's house— everything. I'd rather lose it all than keep it on terms that will help Croyden Roth extend himself.'

Outrage put a fluttering in the banker's flabby cheeks. In the stillness that followed Gwen's impassioned speech he let all his frustration and vindictiveness show. The silence ran out when Judge Gore shifted his shoulders, rustling cloth, settling the hang of his coat, getting stiffly to his feet.

'It should be plain enough that we're getting nowhere,' Gore said. 'I suggest we put an end to it.'

Still quivering with fury, Chaffee pushed back his chair. Rising, he picked up the unsigned note. Deliberately he crumpled the paper in his pudgy hand and dropped it into a wire basket beside the desk. Without looking at Gwen Marshall he circled the desk, flung open the door and marched out into the darkened bank. The Judge followed him.

Roth had his own anger in check. He gave Gwen a mocking bow that invited her to precede him. But when she started to go past, he halted her with words spoken only loudly enough for her ears. 'One last thing, Mrs. Marshall. If you please.'

'Well?'

'I do not like to see anyone making trouble for himself, Mrs. Marshall. Nor do I like the need of resorting to threats. But when I make a verbal contract, I expect it to he honored.'

This time he let her wait.

'That's a very handsome little boy you have, Mrs. Marshall,' he went on quietly. 'A manly little chap. I like him. I'd hate to think of anything that might happen to harm a lad like that.'

That reached her. He saw the flicker of her eyes, the sudden apprehension that drew in her cheeks and seemed to shake her whole body. Her pale lips parted. They stirred to the effort at speech, but achieved no sound.

She went by him, then, in a blind rush to be away from his presence, and Roth let her go, knowing he had said enough. He had pierced the one vulnerable part of her armor. He followed her out into the bank, to the front door which Chaffee had unlocked. Holding the panel open, the banker said tentatively, 'Did you want to—talk about any other matter while you're here, Mr. Roth?' His glance flickered without much hope toward the breast pocket where he had seen that thirty thousand dollar draft deposited.

Roth merely shook his head, dismissing him. He walked out into the spring evening, his thoughts already moving ahead with the program that had received an unexpected rebuff. It was no irreparable one. Yet it occurred to him that it might be a very good idea to assign someone to keep an eye on the Marshall woman—until she broke under her pressures and realized she must come to terms.

He was reaching absently for his cigar case when the step sounded beside him. He turned to find the Judge at his elbow. Henry Gore was a small man, a silent-moving man. He tilted his goat face upward and his thin-boned hand stroked that ruff of whiskers.

'Well, Roth?' he said. And, as the cattleman brought out the leather case and opened it: 'None of your cigars, thanks. They're too expensive a habit for me. I'd rather hear some assurance that you still know what you're doing.'

184

Roth replaced the cigars in his pocket without taking one. 'Are you beginning to think I don't?' he said coldly.

'I'm wondering a little. You've been riding a pretty high horse since you showed up here and talked me into going along with your scheme. Now it looks like things could blow up in your face—and leave Chaffee, me, all of us in trouble.'

Distaste for this blackleg jurist crawled through Roth, and it edged his reply with sharp contempt. 'Look friend, if you went along with me it was because it suited you. Sam Hazen had been riding you hard for years, on account of your double dealings and crooked politics. You were just looking for a way to break him, and I showed promise of doing it. Well, Hazen's dead—but meanwhile you're already in too deep to back out on me or give me trouble, and you know it.'

'Keep a civil tongue when you talk to me!' the old man said raspily. But a moment later the crustiness went out of him and clear worry replaced it. 'You still think you're on top of this thing? In spite of the Marshall woman?'

'Certainly. Just give me time. And don't start moaning before you're hurt.'

Gore clawed at his straggling beard. 'I'd like things a little better,' he admitted, after a moment, 'if I knew for certain we were rid of that Branch Kindred. Cliff shouldn't have let him go. He's a dangerous man. How do we

185

know he won't change his mind about leaving? How do we know he won't be showing up again at some crucial time?'

The question reminded Roth of Bart Hooker. By now, Hooker would already have carried out his orders. Hooker was absolutely dependable. The thought made him smile a little, and he said on an almost genial note, 'That, my friend, is one thing you have no need to worry about.'

CHAPTER TWELVE

The gunman said, 'This is far enough.'

Kindred eased his horse to a stand, and the pair behind him did likewise. A nighthawk swooped past, black against the sky. The trees stood around them with tops silvered by the new-risen moon, and enough of this white shining filtered down to bring out the shapes and contours of the glade among the pines. Kindred waited, listening to a stir of stomping hoofs and rattling of bit chains and the breathing of the horses. The unseen guns at his back were a presence that he could feel, almost like the cold steel of their muzzles against his spine.

'Turn around,' Hooker said.

Carefully he edged the roan about. The two men were there, close. They had moved up the minute he cleared town, and once in timber country, where the prisoner might make a break into the brush and shadows, they had been right at his pony's heels. He would have taken any slight chance they offered him, but Bart Hooker had been too canny for that. And so, having waited in vain for his opportunity, Kindred had waited too long.

They sat motionless in their saddles, faces shadowed beneath hatbrims. He said, 'What do you do after you kill me? Cut off my ears and take them back to Roth for proof?'

'Won't need any proof,' Bart Hooker drawled. 'Roth knows that when I come back from a job it's finished.'

'Someday, there may be a job you don't come back from.'

The gunman seemed to consider this. He lifted his gaunt shoulders in an indifferent shrug. 'Nobody wins all the time.'

'And this,' the second man told Kindred, 'is your turn to lose, mister.'

'Nothing personal in it, of course,' Hooker said affably. 'I hope you understand that. I always did like the kind of man that goes down fighting. It just happens we had to turn up on opposite sides of the fence.'

'Thanks,' Kindred said drily. 'It's a pleasure to know that the one that murders you doesn't hold any grudges.'

That drew a chuckle from the man. Moonlight shimmered on steel as his laughter shook the muzzle of the leveled gun. 'That's what I mean about you, Kindred. You got a sense of humor. I got one myself.'

Numbly Kindred waited and wondered which of the two guns would be the first to fire. At this range, they couldn't help but shoot him dead—unless they chose to gutshoot him and let him die slowly. Rebellion shook him. He measured the distance between himself and those leveled guns. Better to die trying to escape, or grappling for possession of a weapon, than just sit here and take the bullet. He tensed, ready for the try, and then a voice spoke from the trees behind Roth's men.

'There's a double-snouted shotgun ready to blow a tunnel clean through you, Hooker. Try that for a laugh!'

Kindred's breath caught in his lungs, as he recognized the voice of Milt McCune. Unable to see the faces of his enemies, he knew that they had frozen in their saddles. A shotgun was a deadly thing to have at your back.

And yet, even as hope began to pound wildly in his breast, Kindred could anticipate canny Bart Hooker's probable line of reasoning. If McCune was intent on a rescue, he wouldn't be able to use that gun. The figures in the moonlit trail were too tightly bunched. The scatter pattern of a shotgun's shell would sweep them all, indiscriminately, if Milt had to fire. And that locked Milt's trigger finger unless Kindred could do something to break the deadlock.

Do something fast . . .

He hardly took time to think. Milt's shout had rattled his guards, thrown them off balance, diverted their attention. Hooker was beyond his reach, but the other man had crowded a shade too close. Kindred lunged, with a kick of his boot that drove the roan forward.

The gunman yelled and tried to pull away, but Kindred's groping hand found the moon-smeared gunbarrel and clamped down on it. His other fist swung at the man's head and struck his shoulder instead, making him reel in the saddle as the horses met broadside with a shuddering crash. Fingers scraped across his cheek. The two locked, grappling for the gun while their mounts shifted under them and the effort to stay in the saddle hampered them both. Out of the tail of his eye Kindred saw the muzzle-flash of Hooker's gun, stabbing toward the trees. In answer, there came the rushing, blooming crash of the shotgun as Milt let one of the twin barrels go.

Because of Kindred he'd had to pull high. The charge passed over the heads of the horsemen in the trail, a spreading pattern that tore the night wide open. Either the noise, or a stray pellet of shot, had its effect on the horse Kindred's opponent sat. Already frightened enough, the bronc gave a squeal and lunged aside like a startled cat. Kindred held on

189

grimly to that gun. He felt himself behind hauled from his saddle. He kicked free of the near stirrup before his boot could be trapped. And then the roan went out from under him and he was spilling heavily to the ground.

But he had the gun.

He landed rolling, with shod hoofs stamping dangerously about him. He threw an arm across his face in instinctive protection, and a steel shoe struck his elbow a glancing blow that numbed the arm clear to the shoulder. In a crazy confusion of dust and noise he caught the flash of Bart Hooker's six-shooter. He heard the blast of the shotgun's second charge but didn't think it took effect.

Then his knees were under him and he pushed himself to a kneeling position. He saw Hooker leaning from the saddle, his gun gleaming and chopping down. Even as he swung up the weapon he'd captured, Hooker's gun blazed and the muzzle-flash blinded him. A hot iron seemed to strike him on the shoulder. Thrown off balance, he caught himself on the elbow of his gun arm and, lying there, he tilted his gun sharply upward and fired.

It was wild, instinctive shooting. He couldn't really see anything but the smeared after-image of Hooker's weapon exploding in his face.

Dazed and nearly choking on dust and powdersmoke, he fought the bucking recoil of the shot. He brought his arm down ready to fire again. But then he held it. His clearing vision showed Bart Hooker leaning grotesquely sideward on the back of his horse. The gunman's body took on a more awkward slant, and then, quite slowly, Hooker slid out of the saddle. He hit the earth with a limp, sodden sound. At the same moment, Kindred heard another horse break into a gallop. He twisted about.

Having lost his gun and seen Hooker fall, the other Roth gunman was spurring away, bent low and flailing his bronc with his hand. Kindred could have fired but he didn't. The deceptive shadows claimed the fleeing rider. He would not come back.

He climbed to his feet as Milt McCune came running out of the trees, carrying his shotgun and swearing sulphurously.

'Shoulda got 'em both,' Milt accused himself. 'Damn it, I just couldn't seen to hit nothing with this fool Greener!'

'You saved my neck,' Kindred said. 'That's enough for me.' He stood spread-legged in the road, wondering when the giddy world would stop its slow turntable. 'Did you get hit?' he asked.

'Hell, no. Come nowhere near it.' Milt halted beside the dead gunman and used the muzzle of his shotgun to turn Hooker over. The corpse gave limply to the prodding. 'You sure stopped this fellow's clock for him,

Branch.' He saw Hooker's sixgun lying in the dust and stooped to pick it up.

Kindred said, 'What I want to know is how you happened to show when I needed you.'

'Why, I seen you leaving town with that pair on your tail. I ain't exactly a fool. I'd heard about you bein' in jail on some trumped-up charge, and I knew they must be takin' you out for the slaughter. All I had was this shotgun. Until you got into the brush I couldn't come within close enough range to—hey!' He cut himself off with a startled exclamation. 'That's blood on your coat. You're shot!'

'It's nothing,' Kindred said. His arm was still numb from the shock of the iron hoof. The bullet wound felt like nothing more than a dull, deep burning. The sickness that unsteadied his legs and put nausea in him was the lingering effect of Jay Benteen's slugging fists, and the aftermath of the sure death he had faced minutes ago. His horse, checked by the dropping of the split reins, had not wandered far. Kindred shoved his captured gun behind his waistband and walked over to the roan. It caught the smell of blood on him and tried to shy away, but he got the leathers.

'What do you think you're doing?' McCune demanded. 'You ain't going after Roth?'

'If it's the last thing I ever do. I promised him, Milt.'

'Yeah, and he'll be waitin' for you. Don't you understand? The jasper that got away will

192

take him word that you're loose, and he'll have Benteen and his whole crowd of phony deputies ready. It'll be a matters of who gets to put the first slug in you. Hell, man! Use your head!'

'Let me alone,' Kindred snarled at him.

'At least wait'll I get my own bronc—' Milt broke off as he saw the way Kindred sagged against the side of his horse, in the act of trying to shove his toe in the stirrup. 'That arm must be botherin' you worse than I thought.'

'It isn't the arm.'

Kindred stood there clutching the saddle-horn and hating himself, hating the weakness that he couldn't seem to down. And then he looked at the man he'd killed, lying there in the trail with his face turned to the moon, and his stomach rolled over. He thought he was going to be sick again, though he didn't see how anything could be left in his starved, nauseated belly.

Milt McCune's hands were on him. Milt was saying, 'Come on. Let me help you up.' He dragged himself astride, with the aid of those boosting hands, and got his boots settled into the stirrups. 'Now, hang on,' Milt said. 'I'm takin' you to my place. You need some lookin' after.'

He tried to argue, but got nowhere. He reached for the reins but Milt had them. 'Save your wind,' McCune told him gruffly. 'If you want to commit suicide afterwards, that's your privilege. Right now I'm giving the orders.'

'What about him?' Kindred said. 'We can't just leave him' lying there. We—'

'The hell we can't. His friends know where he is if they want him—and I aim to put distance between us in case they come.'

Kindred quit arguing. The old man led the roan to the place in the trees where he had tied his own ugly, rawboned bay.

*   *   *

Milt McCune's homestead was much like its owner, showing in its clutter and squalor the unmistakable signs of shiftlessness. Things had a way of getting ahead of Milt. A broken gate, a missing shingle, waited in vain for repair while other things broke down around him in a steady process of attrition that he seemed unable to cope with. A well he had started to dig, long ago, stood dry and empty while he continued to haul his water up from the creek. His truck garden was a ruin of weeds and insufficient effort.

Kindred suspected that Milt McCune's whole past had been a succession of such hopeless attempts at homemaking, ugly eyesores that he erected and then abandoned, moving on when they overcame him. Sitting in the dingy shack with its sinkful of dirty dishes and its unmade bunk and its corners clogged with trash, he reminded himself that such had

194

been the background of Gwen's life. She had been rebelling against this when she accepted Bill Marshall's proposal of marriage.

How could you blame her?

You couldn't blame Milt, either. He was what he was, and not apologetic about it—a genial failure, long resigned to his own shortcomings. He offered no apologies for the condition of anything. He cleared off the littered, rickety table and, with the lamp set handy for better light, did a crude but effective job of cleaning and bandaging the bullet crease in Kindred's left shoulder. It was a shallow wound that had already quit bleeding.

'I'd advise you to keep usin' that thing if you can,' McCune suggested as he bound it up. 'Just to keep it from goin' stiff.'

'It isn't too bad,' Kindred said, and slipped into a clean shirt from his roll while Milt set himself to the task of cooking up some beans and meat and warmed-over biscuits, on the stove that stood against the grease-spattered wall. In addition to the food, Milt gave his guest a tincup of coffee laced with whisky, and he straddled a chair backwards to watch Kindred eat.

'Go down all right?'

'Fine,' Kindred said. The food was putting new strength in him, and the whisky helped too. He had eaten almost nothing since morning. Hunger, in combination with the beating Jay Benteen had administered, had

195

come near to putting him under.

They discussed the situation. Kindred had long since downed the first wild impulse to return for a showdown with Croyden Roth. McCune had shown him the wasteful futility of that. 'You get yourself killed,' the old man said bleakly, 'and you ain't going to be any help to nobody.'

'There's not much I can do, alive or dead,' Branch said. 'I haven't got Anchor behind me any longer. All I've got is the promise of jail if I defy Earl Hazen's orders to leave the country.'

'Hazen!' The old man spat in disgust. 'That damn blind fool. Ain't there no way to stop him? You're the one hope he has, if he'd only see it. So, he's thrown you out—and before he's through he'll turn this whole range over to Croyden Roth.'

Milt looked around at his filthy, squalid shack. 'I'm just as glad I got nothin' worth hangin' on to,' he growled. 'What good is it now, for old Sam to have give his life buildin' a ranch like Anchor? Where was the use?'

'It doesn't have to be this way,' Kindred said. 'Roth's only a man. If people like John Drum and Will Spencer and the rest would only come to their senses and stand up to him—'

Milt wagged his big head. 'They won't. It's too late—even if they had you to follow, which they ain't now. Who's nervy enough to buck an army of killers, totin' law badges? All at once Roth has the bank, the Judge, the sheriff's office.' Milt grunted mournfully. 'All of them and his toehold on the Dumont Section. And for that, I know who's to blame. Me! Because, Gwen is what I made her.' He looked down at his big hand, lying on the table—the hand that was a futile instrument of a futile will, useful only for the inconsequential rites of whittling, inept at every other chore it had ever undertaken. With a grimace of deep distaste, he clenched the hand into a fist.

And then, suddenly, he lunged to his feet. A gust of breath against his cupped palm blew the lamp, plunging the cabin into darkness. Magically the windows became bright squares of moonlight, and behind the house, one of the horses in the corral repeated its shrill trumpeting.

'Something's in the trees by the creek,' McCune whispered, from the position he had taken at the window. Kindred joined him there, holding the gun he'd captured from Roth's man. 'How could they track us, Branch?'

'Maybe they didn't. Maybe your voice gave you away, back there on the trail.' Kindred cursed himself. 'This is fine repayment for saving my hide.'

Milt didn't even answer that. Kindred heard the scrape of metal against the wall. The old man had picked up his shotgun, which had stood, reloaded, beneath the window. A step carried him to the slab door, and he eased it open. The night's cool breath reached them, carrying the dampness of the creek and—distinctly, now—the sound of an approaching rider.

An exclamation broke from McCune. He flung the door wide, as the horse broke into the moonlit open. 'Gwen!' he said, and then Kindred, too, recognized the slight figure in the saddle. 'She never comes here! And she's got the boy with her!'

Milt leaned his shotgun against the wall and hurried out. Kindred followed him. In confusion and growing alarm, Kindred watched Gwen pull rein, and then he stepped forward to take the bridle and bring the blowing horse to a stand. Gwen was wearing jeans and a shirt, and a jacket that might have belonged to her husband, since it was much too big for her. Milt reached to take the little boy and set him on his chubby legs. Then his hands were at his daughter's waist and Gwen came down from the saddle. She was sobbing.

'Honey!' the old man said hoarsely. 'What is it?'

'It's Billy! Croyden Roth and I had a scene. He—he threatened Billy!'

'The hell he did!'

'He told me if I didn't do exactly what he said—oh, Dad, I'm frightened!' She buried her face against her father's chest.

For a moment, McCune stood perfectly still. Even in the moonlight Kindred could read the incredulous wonder in his face. 'And—you came to me?' Slowly, Milt's arms came up and encircled her, drawing her close, awkwardly patting her shoulder. 'There, there,' he said huskily, as one would comfort a child.

He laid his cheek against her hair, and it seemed to Kindred that he stood taller, straighter, drawing from his daughter's new need of him a dignity and self-respect that were strange and new. Kindred found himself deeply touched by this scene of reconciliation.

Billy came running to him. He scooped the boy up, and then he said, 'What happened between you and Roth?'

Gwen noticed him for the first time. 'Why, Branch! They told me you'd left the country!'

'They were a little previous about *that*,' McCune said drily. 'But Roth, now. We're waitin' to hear, girl. What's your trouble with him?'

'There was a meeting at the bank, Dad. I told him and Frank Chaffee that the deal for the Dumont Section was off.'

'Good girl!'

'Hold on a minute,' Kindred broke in. 'What about the note you owe?'

Gwen made a throw-away gesture. 'Chaffee will do what he wants to about that, I suppose. It doesn't matter.'

'It matters plenty! Are you saying—'

'Now *you* hold it,' Milt McCune said. 'We'll do no good standing around out here talking. Take the boy inside. I'll see to the horse.'

As if she suddenly remembered something, Gwen whirled to clutch his arm and stop him. 'There isn't time to talk at all, Dad. I may have been followed. They were watching the house, after Roth made his threat. I took Billy and sneaked out the back way—'

'You really think there may be someone behind you?' Kindred broke in sharply. He caught her frightened nod. He said, 'Here!' and handed the boy to Milt McCune. He hurried to the corral where both their horses stood tied to a post, still saddled.

His hurt shoulder pulled as he lifted himself astride. Otherwise he felt tolerably well now. Without a word he spurred past Milt and the girl and down into the timber, striking the creek bank trail Gwen had followed and turning back along it.

With the stream sliding and gurgling through the shadows close at hand, he rode cautiously, alert for any other sounds. He knew the chances of catching a warning of danger were slim; his own mount's hoofs made almost no noise in the soft loam of the bank. He pulled his gun and carried it in his hand, not relishing the prospect of blundering into an enemy unprepared. Finally, at a point where the dim trail climbed higher above a clot of rock and willow, he drew in and sat with the night wind full against his face, listening.

Almost at once, he caught it—the crisp ring of iron striking stone, somewhere ahead of him. It came and was gone on the instant, but it was all the warning he needed. He didn't know if it meant one rider, or a dozen, but that didn't matter. With Gwen and the boy dependent on him, he could take no chances. He turned his horse, and spurred back the way he had come.

He found the others waiting in front of the shack, just as he had left them. They seemed to guess that he had bad news. Milt McCune met him with the startled question: 'They here?'

'Yeah. Can't tell how many, but even if it's only one or two we can't afford to risk getting pinned down. We'll do better to stay in the open.'

'Right,' Milt agreed promptly. 'That shack of mine is no place to make a stand. Let's pull out.'

'Hand Billy to me.'

Sleepy and a bit cross with the tension he could feel in these grownups, Billy whimpered as McCune passed him up to Kindred. Branch settled the boy comfortably in front of him, speaking quietly, soothingly as he watched the black motte of the creek. Milt helped Gwen back in her saddle, and then picked up his shotgun and turned to his own ugly bronc. 'Let's go,' he said, and swung his horse in the direction of a draw that opened between two low hills behind the homestead.

They hadn't quite reached its cover when a shot cracked behind them. Kindred, twisting about, saw three riders break into the moonlight and come directly after them. He raised the gun, then remembered that he had only four bullets. Trying to shoot from a running horse would only waste them. He followed Milt and Gwen into the shelter of the draw. There was another shot but the bullet was far short, the distance too great.

Overtaking Milt McCune, he shouted, 'Watch our rear. There's three of them.' He took the lead, after that, setting their course beyond the head of the draw, quartering across a tilting shelf studded with the black shapes of cedar, up over the saddle of a ridge into another draw beyond. He knew this country. Their pursuers didn't. He rode downslope here for a little distance, but then cut out toward the yonder bank. Clearing this, he turned upward again. Branches whipped about him as he broke through a belt of pine, sheltering the boy's head against his shoulder.

The horse was beginning to feel the pace and the constant climbing in rough country. He kept pushing it steadily, but he remembered that Gwen's mount had just been ridden hard from town and probably was tiring. At the head of a long slope that stretched, open and moonbright, behind them, he drew rein in the shadow of spilled boulders and waited for Gwen and Milt to bring their blowing horses even with him.

Though they waited out several watchful minutes, they detected no movement at the bottom of the slope. 'I think we've lost them,' Kindred said finally. 'For the time being, at least—they can hardly pick up our trail again by moonlight. But we'll keep pushing.'

He took the reins again. Billy was asleep, curled up with his tousled head against Kindred's chest. Looking at Gwen, he could see the tiredness in her, the draining of strength that fear and anxiety caused. She straightened her shoulders and gamely lifted her head.

'Where are you taking us?' she asked.

'To Anchor,' he said, and kicked his roan ahead.

*　　　*　　　*

Earl Hazen saw the stars swarming like bees in the dark sky. He felt the saddle pitch under him, and clamped an unsteady hand on the horn to hold himself. The lump of molten fire in his belly made him retch and curse feebly: 'The damned cheap whisky you get here!' Once he slid off his horse and dropped full length upon the ground, with enough clear thought left to remember not to surrender his hold on the reins. He lay like that until the chill of the earth worked its way through his body and revived him a little. Feeling better for it, he got back on his feet and with some effort made the saddle again.

He had no idea what time it was when the horse lagged into the Anchor yard with him, but he thought it was late. Consequently, the splash of lights he saw burning in the headquarters buildings surprised him. He drew rein and stared, a little groggily, at the bunkshack and the main house, and the saddle horses and rigs tied to the picket fence in front of the latter. Then, at last, understanding worked through the whisky fog and he remembered.

It's because of old Sam, he told himself. Your father. He's dead—and you killed him.

The thought sobered him, like the touch of a cold hand. And now, as he watched from a distance, the door of the house opened and people began moving down the path to their waiting saddles and buggies. There were men and women, both, and he knew they must be neighbors come to pay their respects as the word spread of the old man's passing. He recognized John Drum and his gaunt wife, big Barney Weil who carried nearly three hundred pounds on his giant frame. These were people who looked on Sam Hazen's errant son with a good deal of contempt, and so he stayed where he was and listened in bitterness to the calling back of voices in the night, and watched them leave. At last the door shut, for keeps, apparently, and the last of the buggies pulled away, and in a new silence Earl rode forward.

One saddle horse remained. Hazen tied his own and opened the gate, and stood a moment under the shadow of the big cottonwoods frowning at the lighted windows of the house.

Wasn't it Branch Kindred's deep voice he'd heard, among the others? And wasn't that Gwen Marshall passing across one of the squares of lampglow? This, he didn't understand. He had come steeled to the ordeal of another scene with Judy. Here was something he hadn't expected. He didn't know how to face it, or what it meant.

When the door swung open again and men stepped out upon the porch, talking, he took the easier way. He drew back, unseen under the heavy shadow of the tree, and let them come down the path toward him. There were three of them—Kindred, Will Spencer who was another of Anchor's neighbors, and that useless loafer, Milt McCune.

'Man,' McCune said to Spencer in a tone of angry disgust, 'have you got no guts at all?'

'All right, Milt,' Kindred rebuked him in a tired voice. 'This sort of talk won't get us anything.'

'Don't single me out, McCune!' Will Spencer said irritably. 'None of the others that were here tonight are any braver than I am. They've got sense enough to know when the

205

odds are too long.'

'Hell!' Milt McCune said, and spat. 'Add your crew to Barney Weil's, and Drum's, and Anchor's eight—'

'And we still won't be enough to buck a score of professional gunmen carrying deputy's badges. Croyden Roth has been too smart for us, I tell you.'

'And now that you've finally woke up to that fact,' McCune retorted, 'you're going to do nothing. Is that what you're saying?'

'I'm not going to rush into a fight without first doing a hell of a lot of thinking about whether there's any chance of winning it! Let's not be hasty, men! Let's sleep on this. Afterward—'

'Yeah,' Branch Kindred said heavily. 'You go on home, Will, and sleep, on it. That's a lot safer than strapping on a gun.'

'Now, wait a minute!' But as quickly as he bristled, Spencer subsided again. He stood a minute longer, as though he would try to raise further arguments. Instead, he clumped stiffly out through the gate and yanked loose the reins that held his horse anchored to the fence. McCune and Kindred watched him swing into the saddle. There, Spencer hesitated. Plainly he didn't like leaving things on this basis and he said, 'Good night. Pay my respects again to Judy Hazen. I'll be here tomorrow for the burying. Meanwhile, if there's anything at all I can do—'

'There's nothin' you can do!' Milt McCune rumbled at him. 'Go on home!' His words stiffened Will Spencer. He wheeled his horse and stabbed it with a spur. As it spurted away, dust lifted and thinned, a silvery glimmer in the moonlight. The drum of hoofs quickly faded under the wash of night wind in the cottonwoods.

'All alike,' Milt McCune said. 'Every damn one of them. Not a single man in the lot that will fight for his rights.'

'You can't blame them,' Branch Kindred answered. 'Roth's got everything on his side— the bank, the law, the guns. Against a combination like that—'

Earl Hazen chose that moment to step from the gathered shadow at the foot of the tree. They both saw him. McCune uttered a grunt of surprise and Kindred broke off in mid-sentence. Hazen faced them and his tongue tried to find the words he had intended to say. They didn't come, and finally Branch Kindred spoke.

'Well, I guess I didn't keep the promise you got from me. I haven't left.'

McCune shifted his lanky length. 'Your good friend Roth sent a couple of his cannons after him, Hazen—just to make sure he didn't get away alive. Between us we had to kill one of 'em. Did you know about that? Did you know,' he added hoarsely, when no answer came, 'what they would have done to my Gwen and her little boy?'

Hazen made a frantic gesture. 'Please!' he groaned.

'Drunk,' McCune said, in a tone of abysmal disgust. 'It figures, damned if it don't! Hazen, I've always counted myself the world's worst excuse for a man—*and* a father! I'm beginning to think, though, that you've actually got me beat.'

Somehow, the charge struck Hazen like a stunning blow—the mere, inconceivable thought of comparing himself with a ne'er-do-well like McCune. And yet, as he opened his mouth to protest, the justice of the thing came home to him. It was no more than the truth. He had done exactly as little for himself, and for Judy, as this shiftless loafer had ever done. As great a failure as a man, and as a father . . .

'Kindred,' he said, 'there's one thing you've got to know. I've broken with Roth. He showed me his true colors tonight. He showed me you've been right, all along. He's moving that herd up to the Lease first thing tomorrow morning. Anchor, and the rest of the range, can go to hell for all he cares.'

He could feel Kindred's stare eating into him. 'Tomorrow,' Branch Kindred said, as though to himself. 'Tomorrow, huh?'

'I don't deserve anything, I guess,' Hazen went on, doggedly. 'But if you're willing to take an apology—to forget, for Judy's sake, what's happened between us—'

'Shut up!' Milt McCune barked. 'Quit interruptin' when Branch here is workin' on something. You got an idea in your head, man?'

Branch Kindred nodded, very slowly.

'Could be, Milt. Let's get in the house and work it over.'

CHAPTER THIRTEEN

Shortly after two o'clock, the Anchor crew was ready to pull out, abiding by the timetable Kindred had established from the knowledge of his men and of these hills and the distance to be covered. Guns and equipment had been checked, and following these preparations the men had managed to get a couple hours of uneasy sleep before Kindred's calm voice brought them out of their bunks. There wasn't much talking. The old cook had a pot of coffee brewed, to fortify them against the night chill. With his own horse saddled and ready, Kindred walked over to the house and saw Earl Hazen's window still dark. He picked up a handful of small stones and tossed them against the glass. After a minute the window creaked up and Hazen said gruffly, 'I'll be right down.'

In this deep hour of the night, to a mind still numbed by insufficient sleep, sounds were

209

oddly unreal things. Branch Kindred stood there beside the house, waiting for Hazen, and listened to the horses stirring in the corral and the strangely muffled voices of his crew. At a time like this, you could not help casting ahead—wondering about the path you'd set, along which of these men would follow you, and knowing there would be violence at the end of it. You were bound to experience the gnawing beginnings of doubt, the questioning as to the right you had to lead other men into a risky program. And yet, there wasn't a member of the crew who would vote to back out, now that the time had come. They were loyal, to the point of any risk.

Light sprang up in the window of the living room, falling across him. He thought Hazen had lit the lamp but then he noticed Gwen Marshall moving about, a robe she had borrowed from Judy pulled close around her. The door opened and she called his name softly. Beyond her, as he climbed the porch steps, he saw Hazen clomping down the stairs from the second floor.

Earl had dressed himself warmly against the cold. He carried a gunbelt awkwardly across his arm, and his face was white and scowling and pinched. Afraid and more than a little hungover, Kindred guessed. Earl shoved past Gwen, headed for the corral. Kindred sighed. What good would Hazen be in the fight that awaited them?

Then he turned back as Gwen slipped out beside him on the porch, drawing the door shut behind her. 'It's time to go?' she whispered.

'Yes.' The low-turned lamp reached them with its glow, showing her face to him as she stood close and looked up at him, anxiously. 'I figure if we keep pushing it will put us at the Lease by dawn. There's a moon, so riding shouldn't be too difficult. How are Judy and the boy?'

'Both asleep, Branch. Judy, poor thing, was exhausted after yesterday.'

'But not you?'

'I'm all right.'

Kindred frowned, hesitant about saying the next thing that was in his mind. But she was a mature person. She would not be easily panicked. So he told her, soberly, 'This matter of leaving you here alone, Gwen. Frankly, I don't much like it. But Bob Poe and the cook will be around. Spuds is too old for a jaunt like tonight's, and Bob hurt his hip in a fall yesterday and can't ride. They can both handle a gun, though.'

'You're worrying because Roth might have trailed Billy and me here,' she said calmly. 'You mustn't worry, Branch. If it comes to trouble, I can use a gun myself.' She added on a note of anxiety, 'But how many riders will this leave you?'

'Tom Grady and Kansas are camped with

211

the herd. We'll pick them up. With Milt and Hazen, that gives us ten.'

'Ten men,' she said, and shook her head. 'To fight a battle for a whole range! It's shameful that Weil and Spencer and the others should hang back!'

'My fault,' he told her gruffly. 'I just couldn't do a good enough selling job. It isn't always easy to make people see what's good for them.'

'I know,' she said. Her hand lifted toward him. 'Branch?'

'Yes?'

But the hand dropped again. What she told him, in an odd tone, was simply, 'Be careful.'

The crew was mounted and waiting. Kindred delayed to give last-minute instructions to Bob Poe who was hobbling about on the fringes, sour-tempered because of his inability to go along. Then he checked the carbine he'd fastened on his saddle, and swung astride. He'd borrowed a holster and belt for the gun he'd taken off Roth's gunman, and it fit a little awkwardly around his hips. He adjusted the hang of the weapon, flexed the arm that threatened to go stiff on him, and asked, 'Everybody ready?'

'Goddamit,' Milt McCune said, from the back of his tireless, tough, awed bronc. 'Lead out!'

Kindred looked at Earl Hazen, but Hazen seemed to be contained in a glum silence, sitting huddled in his windbreaker and staring darkly at nothing. He squared around in the saddle, then, and picked up the reins. A word of command, and the bunch of horsemen went into motion, already stretching out as they followed Kindred out of the ranch yard.

The white disc of the moon was high, now, and it gave a direct sheen of light that cut shadows to a minimum and made riding by night an easier matter. Still, there was a long trail ahead of them—an all-night trail—and they settled to it with little talking. Kindred, setting the pace, held his roan to a steady gait that would help it to last the distance. There was no fog tonight. The pointed spearheads of the pines, wheeling above them, made sharp black outlines against the stars and the white field of sky centered about the moon. There were few night noises—almost no sound except what their horses and saddle-gear made, and the sough of the wind rocking the trees.

And so they climbed, and the night grew colder as the hours dragged out. And as a man will at such time, Branch Kindred found his mind busily, relentlessly working, tracking over the course of events that had led to this, working out the involved relationship of people and problems. When he came to himself and Gwen, he tried to shut these futile obsessions from his mind. In whatever awaited him with daybreak, he would need a clear head

213

and quick responses. Such thoughts as these could do him little good.

He called a halt for the second time, to dismount and rest their horses. Ed Farrar came to him and said, 'Hazen's disappeared.'

'What!'

'Bastard snuck out on us,' Farrar said bleakly, 'some time since the last stop. I just happened to look for him and he's gone. I don't think anyone else realizes it yet. What do you think, Branch? Is he off to warn Roth what we're up to? It wouldn't be the first time he double-crossed us.'

Kindred considered the question. It was a tremendously important one. On his estimate of Earl Hazen and his reasons for deserting the column, depended the wisdom of continuing with this program—of asking these decent cowboys to follow him into something that might or might not prove another trap.

He said, 'I don't think that's it, Ed. Not this time. I think, at last, Hazen knows the straight of Croyden Roth.'

The puncher gave a snort. 'Then he's turned coward on us. And it ain't surprising to me. Why, he was plum shakin' in his boots when he come down to the corral. I thought it might have been the likker backin' up on him—but I guess it was just plain yellowbelly. And so,' he added savagely, 'the skunk is lettin' us go without him, to fight to save his ranch!'

'What I'm doing,' Kindred told him, 'is for

Sam—and for Judy!'

Farrar didn't answer that. But finally he said, 'Earl would be damn little use to us anyway, I guess. The hell with him. Last night, though, I had an idea he'd been shamed into trying at least to *act* like a man.'

Kindred, didn't say so, but he shared Ed Farrar's sentiments. He had wanted to believe better things of Hazen. He felt disappointment, keenly, for Judy's sake. But they'd known what Earl Hazen was, and he lifted his shoulders in a shrug.

'Give the word to mount up again, Ed. We aren't making as good time as I'd counted on.'

Suddenly, day came on with a rush.

Kindred watched the gray stain of light strengthening, the world taking on a hint of color, and he fidgeted and cursed silently, feeling an anxiety he wouldn't show his men. They had cut it a shade too fine. It had taken perhaps half an hour longer than he had counted, and now the moon hung far over in the west and the mule-ear portals of the Dumont Lease showed above them with increasing clarity, as they waited silently in the fringe of the timber.

Looking around him, Kindred could begin to make out the faces of the men. They all showed the strain of anticipation, and of the sleepless night. He saw Sid Novak start to pull out tobacco sack and papers, then give it up and shove them back into his shirt pocket. Sid

215

was thinking you couldn't be too careful. He probably wanted a smoke the worst way, but in the pre-dawn quiet the drift of burning tobacco might carry a long distance—even as far as that spur of rocks within the entrance, where a guard would be stationed if there was a guard.

That was a point that had to be settled before they could move another yard, and young Tom Grady had volunteered for the chore of finding out. He had mountain goat in his family tree, Tom insisted, and he could without any trouble find a way up that ridge, above the flat-iron slabs, and so get into a position to search the lookout and make certain if anyone was there. Kindred had finally let him go, first exacting a promise that the kid would do no more than establish the fact. And the kid had promised that he'd leave it to Kindred to devise a way to knock the guard out of his nest, taking no chance of alarming him or allowing a gunshot that would alert the entire camp.

But it was hard waiting. The coldest hour of any night, just before sunrise. Kindred's arm hurt with a dull, throbbing ache. He flexed it, exercising the kinks out of it, and watched the steel-gray sky begin to take on a hint of blue.

Then Joe Anderson said, 'Here's the kid,' and with surprising suddenness Grady slipped back among them, grinning at the way he had managed to sneak in on his friends without letting himself be heard or seen until he was on top of them.

'Told you I was light-footed,' he said. 'The half of me that ain't mountain goat is Injun.'

'All right,' Ed Farrar said impatiently, his breath a misty plume spurting from his lips. 'What about the guard?'

'Ain't any. No sign of one.'

'You're sure of that?' Kindred demanded. He questioned Tom carefully, and was finally satisfied. The kid had had a good gander at the whole section. He'd seen horses grazing near the cabin, a pick-up bronc in the corral. But the lookout spot was deserted. Grady was certain of that.

'Them cannons of Roth's are so dangerous they figure they're safe,' Milt McCune suggested. 'They got away with their bluff yesterday and they won't be lookin' for anybody to walk in on them now. They're down at the cabin in their blankets, snoring.'

'But not for much longer,' Kindred said. 'It'll be daylight in another half hour. We'll have to take the risk and hope that we're lucky, because we haven't time to do anything else. Let's move in.'

They left the trees and rode up across a steep open toward the gap. They didn't need to be told to spread out, making a poorer target in case Grady had made a mistake. Kindred pulled his belt gun and laid it on his thigh. There was a tightness all through him. It

217

seemed that the slowly moving horses were making noise enough for a troop of cavalry. Yet he knew his nervousness was not personal fear, but the responsibility of a leader for the men who followed him.

They came through the gap and nothing happened. The park stretched ahead of them, as quiet as Grady had reported. Kindred lifted a hand to halt the line, and studied the pile of rocks where the man with the rifle had stopped him yesterday. He turned to Grady, with a jerk of his head. 'Up there, Tom. We won't make the same mistake. You keep a lookout—and a good one.'

Grady eyed him in consternation. 'Aw, hell, Branch!' the kid stammered. 'Why *me*?' You could tell that the order had taken the wind out of his sails, inflated as they'd been by the success of his scouting mission. He plainly believed that Kindred was treating him now as the baby of the outfit, deliberately putting him out of danger. But he was too proud to say this, and as it happened he was exactly right. Kindred returned his rebellious stare, without yielding. And Grady yanked his horse out of the line and proceeded in poor grace to do as he'd been told.

With seven men behind him now, Kindred rode onto the Lease.

The light grew steadily stronger. They skirted the edge of the lake, that lay steaming and silent under the brightening sky. A horse, grazing the rich growth beside the water, lifted its head to watch them by. Over at the cabin, there was no movement at all except for the single catchup horse in the trap, that came to the bars and watched the newcomers ride in. Kindred kept a careful eye on the closed door, but when they came within a dozen feet of the building without raising a bullet he believed that all was still well. If those inside weren't asleep, they would never have let an enemy get in this close.

He brought the line to a halt, signaling his men to spread out. Joe Anderson swung wide to disappear behind the building, where there was a storage lean-to with a second door. The shack had only one window, and Sid Novak was watching that intently with a gun ready to shoot the first thing that moved at it.

Just then the lone horse in the corral let loose with shrill, trumpeting blast.

Kindred raised his gun and waited for the first warning of an aroused response within the shack. A minute passed, and another. He forced his nerves to loosen and deliberately, then, he heeled his roan forward. At a walk he drew in while his men waited, in a circle about the building. He advanced to within a scant three yards from the slab door. Suddenly it jerked open and a man stepped out in undershirt and jeans and sock feet, carrying a carbine by the balance.

He directed his attention toward the corral,

and the disturbance there that had wakened him. He didn't seem to notice the ring of riders, even when his sleep-fogged stare rested on them. But then Kindred saw awareness shock through the man, saw his eyes go round and his mouth open and the carbine leap toward firing position. He spurred straight at him.

The roan slammed full-tilt into the man, knocking him back against the house and blocking the rise of the long gun. It couldn't still the shout of alarm, but that didn't matter. The barrel of Kindred's revolver rose and descended sharply, and the man crumpled like a wad of rags.

There was no time to wonder if he'd crushed the skull with that chopping blow. The cabin had come alive, magically, and it was a matter of moving fast and taking advantage of whatever surprise was still left. Recklessly Kindred hurled himself out of the saddle, striking the half-closed door with his shoulder. As it went wide he heard the confused shouting of voices within and the blast of a room-trapped shot. He braced himself to take a bullet but no lead met him.

He saw then that he hadn't been the target. Joe Anderson had beaten him in, likely tearing open the storage room door on the instant of hearing a warning shout out front. A blanket hung in the doorway of that rear lean-to. Now, in a single shocked glance, Kindred saw the

Anchor puncher falling, clutching at the blanket and bringing it to the floor with him. Out of the tail of his eye he saw the gun that had shot Joe. One of Roth's men lay propped on an elbow in his bunk, and he had the smoking weapon ready to put a second bullet after the first. Kindred didn't give him the chance. Almost without thinking, and without taking aim, he swung his gun and fired and the man let out a scream of pain, and dropped in a sprawl half out of the bunk.

There were three others in the cabin, one in the room's remaining bunk and the other pair scrambling, startled, out of the blankets they'd spread on the floor. None had laid his gun very far from his hand, and they were grabbing for them now, as they stumbled to their feet. One threw a shot at Kindred. It missed because he fired too fast and was still tangled in his blankets. Kindred, sidestepping out of the open doorway, swung his sixgun and tried to shout an order to hold fire, but his voice was lost in a sudden smash of glass. Sid Novak, reining in close to the window, had leaned from saddle to poke his rifle through the pane.

A gun roared deafeningly. There was a grunt as someone following Kindred through the door took a slug. Kindred and Novak triggered at the same instant. Both their shots hit, for the man who had fired jerked insanely with the bullets riddling him from two directions, and collapsed.

As suddenly as it started, it ended. All at once the cabin filled with Anchor men and the remaining pair of Roth gunfighters were ready enough to throw down their weapons. Dazed still by the shock of their waking and the overwhelming completeness of surprise, they stood and let themselves be surrounded. 'Tie them up,' Kindred said, and pouched his gun as he turned to see how it went with his own men who had been hurt.

The old puncher known only as 'Kansas' had taken the bullet meant for Kindred. He sat on the floor staring at the bloody mess a shallow streak across his ribs was making of his hickory shirt. Joe Anderson's hurt was more serious—a bad hip wound that fountained blood with every pulse beat. Milt McCune laid aside his shotgun and said gruffly, 'Get out of the way and let me work on him before he bleeds to death,' and Kindred let him have his way.

One of the Roth men was dead, with two bullets in him. The one in the bunk was groaning over a smashed arm. The man who'd gone out to investigate the disturbance at the corral would be some time recovering from the blow with the gunbarrel that Kindred had dealt him. Five of the enemy had been eliminated, at a cost of injuries to two Anchor riders. So far, the results were grimly satisfactory. But this counted no more than the first round.

The smell of burnt powder slowly cleared from the room, on a cross draft of dawn wind between open door and broken window. Outside, the flush of dawn brought life into the waking world. 'Somebody pass the signal to Tom Grady,' Kindred ordered. 'He'll be getting pretty anxious.'

'And after that, what happens?' someone asked.

'After that,' Kindred said, 'we wait.'

CHAPTER FOURTEEN

The waiting was hard, and they had a lot of it to do. Computing the hour at which Roth might be expected to move his cattle off the herd ground, and the rate at which he would be able to push them in these unfamiliar hills, Kindred knew it must be late afternoon before he could expect to see sign of them. Roth might even take two days to make the drive, although this he frankly doubted. For all the man's colossal assurance and the seeming completeness of his success Roth wouldn't deliberately invite attack. By nightfall he'd want his herd safe on the Section, where it could be defended.

So the Anchor crew settled down to a lengthy vigil. The body of the dead gunman was removed, and the wounded treated with

223

such materials as could be found in Jake Dumont's cabin. They cooked a meal, and afterward Sid Novak rode out to relieve Tom Grady on watch and let the kid come in for his grub. Someone found the inevitable deck of line-camp Bicycle cards and a game started, but no one had much mind for it.

Plowing through the supplies in the storage lean-to, Milt McCune turned up a nearly full tin of kerosene. This gave Milt an idea, and without consulting anyone he set to work on a project that involved torn-up blankets and pine chunks that he took from the woodbox. Kindred guessed what was in his mind and let him alone. The old man, with harsh realism, had hit upon something that would probably stand them in good stead before this business was over—maybe split the odds against them and spell the difference between defeat and victory.

And so the hours dragged on, weighted with the oppression of sitting idle. It had turned warm, and the prickly itch of perspiration helped to roughen tempers that were already rubbed raw by the dragging file of time. Branch Kindred found himself considering a hundred prodding questions, a hundred doubts as to the wisdom of his tactics. He thought about Gwen and Judy, alone at Anchor with only Bob Poe and the cook for protection. Supposing he had guessed Roth's intentions wrongly? What if some dark purpose sent the man there while the Anchor crew waited in vain for him in the hills?

He was pacing before the cabin, fighting his fears, when Milt McCune came out to join him. They walked together in silence, the young cowman and the gaunt old farmer stumping along in his worn jackboots. For a while neither spoke, watching the sheen of fir needles in the sun, and the sparkles on the lake where a pair of wild mallards paddled.

'Some of your boys are gettin' kind of touchy,' McCune said at last. 'It's this settin' around with nothin' to do and plenty of time to think. They feel it.'

'Yes,' Kindred agreed.

'And they're thinkin', too,' the old man said, 'about the men that should be here and ain't. Especially, they're cussin' that no-good that run out on us, on the way up. I know how they feel. It makes me wonder a little just what in the name of sense *I'm* doin' here.'

Milt took a few paces without speaking.

'Then,' he went on, 'I find myself wonderin' something else. Suppose Hazen run to Croyden Roth again? Suppose he told Roth about us takin' off for the hills—and my Gwen at the Anchor place, and Billy, too. Hell, mister! Gwen's the key to the whole situation. If Roth happens to be set on layin' hands on her—' He broke off, unable to finish.

'I know, Milt. I've had that thought.' Kindred wondered if his voice betrayed his

225

inner tension. 'But somehow I don't believe Earl Hazen has turned his coat a second time.'

McCune shrugged hunched shoulders. 'We can only hope you're right.' He shot a sidewise look at Kindred. 'If you are, Branch, an' if we all get through this thing, what about you and Gwen?'

'What do you mean?' The words were jarred out of him.

'I got an idea,' the old man said bluntly, 'that you still think about that girl. I'm askin' if you love her enough to take her second hand? With another man's son into the bargain?'

There could be only one honest answer, and Kindred gave it. 'I'd ask her in a minute. That's the truth, Milt. But—why should I think she'd have me, this time? I haven't changed and in three years.'

'Maybe *she* has,' the old man said.

And then a drum of hoofbeats, bearing toward them from the direction of the gap, claimed their whole attention.

'It's the kid,' McCune said. 'I reckon we're for it, Branch.'

Too restless for waiting, Tom Grady had asked permission to ride down the trail to a point where he could spot approaching riders sooner than Sid Novak could from his lookout. Now here he came tearing back, pressing his mount hard, and Kindred knew that Milt was probably right.

'Might as well tell the boys to get ready,' he

said. But someone in the cabin must have seen Grady through the window, because even as Kindred spoke the door swung open and his crew came rushing out. Bill Hirsh held a poker hand that he hadn't bothered to lay down.

Grady brought his horse back on its haunches, steelshod hoofs gouting sod. 'Get your guns!' he shouted, and made a wide and sweeping gesture. 'Here they come!'

'Just what did you see?' Kindred demanded.

'Their dust. It's strung out for miles, coming right up the trail. And I spotted that Benteen hombre, ridin' scout. I never let him see me.'

'How far are they?'

'A couple miles below the gap, anyway.'

'All right. Good work, Tom. Kindred turned to the crew. 'Mount up!'

They began a sober and orderly movement toward the corral and the waiting horses. Kindred had already overridden the strong protests of Kansas and Joe Anderson with orders that the hurt men were to stay behind and keep a guard on the prisoners. That left five riders besides himself and Milt McCune, against whatever crew Roth might have seen fit to bring along. And, knowing that his herd would be vulnerable to any attack while they were strung out helplessly on the trail into the hills, Roth likely had brought the bulk of his gunmen. It was what Kindred would have done in his place.

Half a dozen guns were not many, to close a

quartermile gap against a thousand head of cattle and a dozen or more determined riders. Because of the steep, slick faces of flatiron rock that flanked the opening, Kindred had little chance of placing his men strategically to create an ambush. The gap was wide and open and scarcely defensible. They would have to stand and meet the Roth bunch and drive them back as best they could.

In the long run, the outcome of this business might rest with old Milt McCune, who brought up the rear now with bundles of pine kindling and torn blankets beneath his arm and the tin of kerosene sloshing on his saddle.

Novak, in the lookout, was wigwagging frantically. Kindred returned the signal to show that he understood. As they came into the gap he could see the thin haze of dust drifting across the timber below. The nearing herd was making good time. Already, an updraft of air brought the faint sound of their mingled, lowing mutter.

'All right,' Kindred said. 'Space out. Keep your guns ready and wait for my word.'

Scowling, Ed Farrar said, 'You don't really think a piece of paper can stop a man like Croyden Roth?'

'Probably not. Still, it's the only shred of legality we can bring against that assortment of special deputy badges his men are wearing. He's got to know at least that the shoe's been on the other foot since yesterday morning.

Whatever happens afterward will be his responsibility.'

To forestall further argument, he rode out alone through the gap, drawing rein at the head of a long, open slope of bunch grass that fell away toward a fringe of lower timber where the drive trail, long used by Anchor's herds, broke out of the trees. He took out his belt gun, checked it and slid it carefully back into the leather, not shoving it deep but letting it ride light for a quick draw. He tested the slide of the carbine in its scabbard under his knee. And then he straightened, shoulders stiffening, as he saw a rider drift into the open below him.

The distance was too great for recognition. The horseman must have taken it for granted the motionless figure at the head of the slope was one of his own kind, for he came on without hesitation. Sunlight winked from the metal trappings of his gear, from spur rowel and bit chain and cartridge-studded belt. And then, suddenly, the Roth gunman sensed something wrong. His head jerked up, the shadow of the wide-brimmed hat sliding from his face. The horse braked, to the pull of the reins.

Behind him, movement sifted through the belt of fir timber. Kindred saw red hides among the dark trunks, heard the bellowing of the herd as the lead steer came plodding into the open, with the point of the drive at its tail.

A second rider broke through the film of hoof-raised dust. The first one turned his head and barked a warning, and Kindred saw the other man react to it.

Deliberately, then, he touched heel to his horse, and the tight curb he held on the reins made the roan move under him in a narrow circle—plains Indian sign language for a parley. While the men below watched, he rode the circle a second time. After that he lifted his right hand clear, and started boldly down the slope. Obviously they had understood his signal, for the first rider kicked his horse and came slowly on to meet him. The other man stayed put, but he slid a sixgun from its holster and held it across his knee. The point of the herd, pushed ahead by the animals behind it, lumbered slowly on into the open.

Roth's man and the Anchor foreman approached each other cautiously, and halted. The gunman searched the gap briefly, and finding nothing there, concentrated on Branch Kindred.

'What the hell are you doing here?' he asked. 'And what's become of the men we left?'

'That's something I'll talk over with your boss,' Kindred said. 'Is Roth with you?'

'Yeah. Back down the trail a piece.'

'Fetch him.'

'Why the hell should I?' But the gunman's belligerent edge was dulled by uncertainty, and by an authority he seemed to read in Kindred's cool steadiness. He scowled blackly, but then he yanked his horse around and went back down the slope.

Kindred lowered his right hand carefully, placed it together with his left upon the saddle-horn. He saw the gunman pause to exchange a word with the second rider, who had come no farther than the edge of the trees. He disappeared, then, and another period of waiting began—the kind that could draw out a man's nerves like fine thread wire. The afternoon sun bore down heavily. Kindred felt sweat track a course over his ribs, and his arm ached dully. Behind him, only silence. That rider at the foot of the slope sat and watched him, and the cattle, no longer held in line, began to scatter out and fall to graze on the thin bunch grass that clung to this loose soil. More cattle kept coming up the trail, continuing to spill out into the open. The constant lowing was like the muffled booming of a surf.

Suddenly Croyden Roth appeared astride a big, handsome bay. Two of his men followed hard behind. They halted, looking up at Kindred. Roth gave a command and his riders fell back. Then he spurred ahead, pushing a way through the growing mill of the stalled drive. He came directly toward Kindred, and his mouth was a hard, sharp slash.

Roth reined in with a savage pull that made

the bay toss its head, and just stared at Kindred while he fought down the roiling tempers within him. Kindred had never seen this man beyond control, but he suspected he was close to seeing it now.

'Remember,' Kindred said, 'I told you we'd be meeting again, one way or another.'

Roth's mouth corners twitched. 'What's happened to the crew I left up here?'

'They'll live to hang, some day. All but one. He's dead.'

'I don't know how you managed this, Kindred. But I hope you haven't forgotten he was a deputy sheriff, acting in the line of duty.'

'That injunction, you mean?' Kindred reached into his shirt pocket. 'I've got a paper of my own,' he said, bringing it out. 'I think you should have a look. This is a renewal of Anchor's lease to the Dumont Section. It has the signatures of Gwen Marshall and Earl Hazen. Want to verify them?'

Roth made no move to take the paper. 'I've never seen their handwriting. I'll take your word.'

'That's sensible,' Kindred said, and stuffed the paper back again. 'You see, Roth, even you can make a mistake. You kick too many people around once too often, and they're apt to join and turn against you.'

He picked up the reins in his left hand, leaving his right hanging free. 'This paper changes things a little between us. It nullifies that court order. Bring your crew and your cattle onto this section, and you're the one who'll be trespassing. Better think it over.'

Their stares locked for a long and challenging moment. Then Branch Kindred wheeled his horse and jabbed the spur.

It was a risk, turning his back on a man full of killing hate, and yet, Kindred did not believe that Roth would give way to the temptation. It would be an admission of defeat, a reckless abandoning of any show of legality. He didn't think Roth was ready for that, yet.

He was wrong.

The big man must have read the signs differently. He must have seen clearly enough into the future to realize that defeat stemmed from this moment; that if he let Kindred take and keep the initiative, by sitting idly and letting him ride away, he would forfeit his last chance of winning. Some such reasoning must have worked through Roth's coldly logical brain, causing his hand to move—and bringing to Kindred's ears the faint whisper of metal sliding against leather.

Kindred reacted with desperate speed. A rake of the spur made the roan leap under him as he whipped about, grabbing for his own belt gun. He heard the crack of Roth's weapon, heard the near passing of the bullet. His unaimed answering shot keened off into empty air. He was steadying his mount for a better one when Roth fired again and he felt the jarring impact as the heavy bullet smashed into the body of the roan.

Kindred knew the animal was hard hit, perhaps fatally, from the way it stumbled under him just as he brought his smoking six-shooter down for a second try. He eased off the trigger, to avoid wasting a bullet. At the same instant a saddle gun cracked, down below him. He cast a hurried glance downslope and saw four of Roth's men spurring hard, converging on him, threading a way through the scattering cattle.

A hundred yards stretched between him and the gap. He could only try to make it.

He turned again in the saddle; he yelled at the roan, and the game animal, though dying on its feet, made its response. Rubble gouted as its iron hoofs dug in, Kindred helping as much as he could by throwing his weight forward. Behind him the pound of those nearing horses came up strongly. A gun spoke—whether Roth's or one of the others, he didn't know—and something plucked his hat from his head and sent it kiting. But still he went unhit. He began to think he would ride out their bullets. And then, all at once, the roan went down.

Kindred felt it going. He meant to leap clear, but in the last split second the loose soil twisted the dying bronc sharply sideward. Man and horse fell together, with the whole weight of the roan coming down full on Kindred's left leg. It left him shocked, dazed, knowing he was trapped but unable to move because he'd taken the fall on his hurt shoulder. He heard his enemies' exultant shouts, and above him, a cry of dismay that came from one of his own men as they saw him fall.

A gun roared and a bullet stamped into the barrel of the dead horse. That jarred him into action. Quickly propping himself on his left elbow, he swung up the sixgun that he'd managed to hold onto. It bucked against his hand. Smoke leaped from the muzzle and through it he saw the nearest of the riders go spinning off the saddle. He looked for Roth but failed to find him. At the same time other guns started working from the head of the slope, above and behind him, and that meant his own half-dozen were pitching in to help.

They aimed high, firing downhill with Kindred trapped between them and their targets, but still they managed to turn back the Roth trio who were trying to finish him off. One took a hit and slewed off his horse in the very act of turning it. The remaining pair of killers gave way quickly enough, then, and drew out of range. When the dust cleared Kindred saw that they had retreated clear into the timber, leaving their dead and the bawling, frightened cattle.

And Croyden Roth had vanished with them.

For the moment there was no sign of action

on the slope below. But this couldn't be over. Not yet. Kindred let trapped air out of his lungs. He turned his head as Ed Farrar started down to him, and yelled, 'Stay back. I'm not hurt. I can get out of this.'

Farrar reluctantly obeyed, and Kindred set to work to free his trapped leg.

Right away he realized that he was stuck faster than he'd thought, but luckily, the soil was loose. Bracing his topside boot against the saddle and working until his knee threatened to spring out of joint, he managed to slide the leg nearly free. But just when he believed he had it drawn clear his boot caught on the saddle. The foot wedged hard and all his efforts failed to budge it. He fought himself breathless, and finally he dropped flat to get his wind and ease the ache in his pinioned leg. 'Guess I was wrong, Ed,' he called. 'Maybe you'd better bring a rope down here.'

And at that moment, gunfire erupted down below in the trees. He dragged himself up on his elbows again, not quite sure what was happening. He saw the red-coated herd of cattle pouring blindly out of the timber, and then he understood. Riders—almost a dozen of them—were yelling and brandishing guns and coiled ropes. Their yelling and the racket of their guns was enough to catch up that mill of stalled cattle, quickly weld it into a solid, moving mass—and this they started straight up the slope, toward the entrance of the Lease, toward the man who lay pinned under his dead horse.

Watching them come, he thought his blood had turned to ice. This was Croyden Roth's final bid. He meant to use this herd of his as a gigantic weapon to roll back his enemies, or roll over them. Even as Kindred caught up his gun he knew that mere bullets could not turn back the juggernaut. Nor would Roth care how many head he lost. His goal was possession of the Lease, and once he had it he could defy anyone to push him off it.

Sick with horror, Kindred emptied his remaining shells. With those beeves running shoulder to shoulder, he could hardly miss. A steer went tumbling with each bullet. But the front of the wave just broke and closed solid again, and the earth shook to its swelling thunder. When the hammer clicked on a spent cartridge, Kindred dropped his gun. There was no time to reload.

He remembered his carbine, thrusting from the saddle scabbard. He reached and pulled it out, but as he started to lever a shell into the breech something came sailing over his head, end over end, with a *whoosh*, and a mass of flame. Trailing a black plume of foul-smelling smoke, it landed yards short of the oncoming herd and went rolling and bouncing down to meet them. Kindred had forgotten the torches, improvised by Milt McCune from pinewood and kerosene-soaked blanket! A second blazing brand whizzed over. This one hit the herd leaders squarely and it struck bawling panic from them. Despite the packed pressure behind them, the front ranks split and wildly fell away from it.

Now the whole Anchor crew was tearing recklessly down the slope, risking crippling spills from their horses and the guns that outnumbered them two to one. They all had Milt's homemade grenades and they lighted them and hurled them into the forward ranks of the cattle. They were accomplishing just what Milt had hoped for.

Gunfire and yelling riders could not prevail against this greater terror. The herd had been stopped as though by a brick wall. It turned on itself, and broke, and ceased to be a herd. And Kindred, realizing that the carbine could be a tool as well as a weapon, lowered it unfired and set to work slamming the butt against the ground, chopping powdery dirt away from his imprisoned leg.

Swiftly he tore a shallow furrow and with a last heedless wrench dragged himself free. Cramped muscles buckled and nearly dumped him as he scrambled to his feet. A bronc plowed to a halt, yards distant. Billy Hirsh yelled anxiously, 'Branch! You all right?'

Kindred waved Hirsh on. Leaping the body of his dead mount, he went charging down into the fight with boots kicking long gouges in the loose soil and carbine at the ready.

CHAPTER FIFTEEN

It was all confusion. The cattle panic had become a running scramble. Here and there bunch grass clumps had caught afire. An oily stink and swirl of kerosene smoke mingled with raised dust and carbide smell and the crash of guns and yelling of men. Moving forward, Kindred caught sight of Tom Grady galloping recklessly into the tangle, brandishing one of the flaming torches. The kid leaned out and swung the brand right in the faces of the cattle. He yelled and crowded his bronc ahead, and the terrified steers blatted and bawled and piled up on one another in their frenzy to give way. Kindred had a glimpse of the youngster's face—hatless, tawny hair whipping in the wind, mouth stretched wide, shouting with excitement.

Then all that wild elation washed off the youngster's face. His whole body jerked. He lost torch and reins and the lunging horse buckjumped from under him. Kindred saw him turn in the air and vanish, in a sprawl, amid the ruck of swirling dust and smoke and surging bodies.

A yell broke from Kindred. He swerved in that direction, but hauled when he saw Sid Novak already spurring over to help. Standing there, spreadlegged, he threw a furious searching glance around until he found the man who had shot Tom Grady. It was Jay Benteen. The trail boss caught sight of Kindred at the same moment. The ugly, broken-nosed face twisted with rage. Benteen's gun, still smoking from the shot that had downed the kid, swung sharply.

Kindred slapped the butt of the carbine against his braced hip, brought the barrel around and squeezed trigger. He shot Benteen through the chest and watched him leave the saddle with his gun unfired. Strangely, he felt no emotion at all.

Then a shift of the wind dropped a cloud of oil smoke that filled his throat and stung his eyes and set him coughing, and the crazy confusion around him was lost. Automatically he levered a fresh shell into his carbine, but in the dust and the smoke he could find no target. He saw no more torches being hurled and judged that the last had been used up. Well, they had done their work. There was one herd of cattle that wouldn't be driven onto the Lease today, no matter how many hands Roth had brought with him. Terror had made the cattle utterly unmanageable.

But he had to find a horse.

Almost with the thought, he saw one come pounding toward him out of the pall of dust and smoke. He didn't stop to notice if it was an Anchor mount, or if some Roth man had lost his saddle. He lunged in, and a flopping stirrup narrowly missed his face as he reached for the headstall. Terrified, the animal tried to shy away but he caught the leather and hung on, bringing it to a stand at the cost of nearly jerking his hurt arm from the socket. He spoke to calm the trembling horse, then lifted himself into a saddle that was still warm from another man's body. Exulting, now, he pulled the bronc around and sent it slamming into the fight. Dimly he could hear his own voice shouting Croyden Roth's name.

Steers fled from his path like deer. A rider drifted blackly through the murk and threw a shot at him. He started to return it but held off. How could you tell friend from enemy? As he hesitated, the rider moved on and he let him go. He only wanted one man out of this. Only one.

'Roth!' he shouted in a voice gone hoarse with the dust he'd swallowed. 'Damn you, Roth, *where are you?*'

'Kindred!'

He jerked about, and his hand was tight on the grip and the trigger of his gun. He stared hard, not ready to believe. And yet, there could be no mistaking the bulk of the rider who loomed through the smoke pall. On a specially built saddle, and a massive horse handpicked to carry his nearly three hundred pounds, Barney Weil spurred toward him. Barney fisted a smoking six-shooter and his face was grim and beaded with sweat to which

241

the dust clung thickly. Sweat formed great circles under his arms and across the front of his shirt where the belt pinched it. A saddle was agony for a man as big as Barney Weil. Barney did as much of his range work as he could from the seat of a battered old buggy with a steel reinforced frame.

'Where the hell,' Kindred said, 'did you come from?'

'Why, we're all here,' Weil told him, between gasps for breath. 'Me and Drum and Spencer and our crews. Thank God we made it in time. Or, rather—thank Earl Hazen.'

'Hazen!'

Weil nodded. 'It's his doing. He about killed a bronc, routing us out—bringing word you were headed for the showdown. He said after he'd started up here with your crew he made up his mind that it was our place to be here and if we were too much cowards to listen to a brave man, we just might listen to another coward!' Barney's red sweaty cheeks got redder, but he met Kindred's eyes directly. He said, 'Honest to God, I never knew the man had guts enough to talk up the way he done to me. Made me feel ashamed of myself—and the others too, I guess. Anyway, we came.'

'Hazen's with you?'

'Yonder, somewhere.' Weil jerked his massive head and Kindred became aware of increased gunfire rolling across the smoke-drifting slope. 'We're mopping up. Tough as

242

they are, that crew wasn't expecting anyone to hit them from behind.'

'What about Roth? Have you seen him?'

'No.' Barney Weil shouted it across his shoulder. He was already pulling his horse around, spurring back into the smoke, gun held high and great bulk swaying perilously in the saddle. Kindred started hard after him, over the hoof-churned ground. But then something made him pull rein and consider, his smarting eyes narrowed with impatience and doubt. He ran a palm across his jaw, and felt the itchy rasp of day-old beard.

He just couldn't believe that Roth would let himself be caught in a trap. The hill ranchers had come in behind him, and it sounded as though they'd converted the whole southwest end of the slope into a battlefield. Roth could scarcely have got through the gap in back of Kindred, without Kindred knowing. It left one direction open—the north, where the land tilted up into a spur of broken rock and heavy timber.

Suddenly Kindred remembered the shadowy figure which had gone drifting past him in the dust fog, and the shot he hadn't risked answering, for fear of putting lead into one of his own men. And without knowing why, he felt very certain that the man had been Croyden Roth, seeking escape from a fight gone wrong.

He pulled his horse around and sank the

spurs. The unfamiliar animal—it couldn't be an Anchor mount—tried to buck but he held it down with a firm hand and got it straightened out. He swung it in the direction he believed Roth had taken, and sent it that way at as hard a pace as he could chance.

Very quickly he rode out of the dust and smoke. Beyond lay open ground, tilting sharply up toward the nearest timber. Kindred scanned it but detected no movement. He was alone, and with the guns firing at his back there came a temptation to believe that he'd made a mistake—that he belonged back there with his men, in the thick of the fighting. He cursed, started to drag his horse around again. And then he saw the single set of prints, leading ahead.

A bronc's hoofs dug deep and clear, in this loose soil. This one was a big horse, ridden hard. He remembered that big bay of Roth's. It could have made such tracks.

That did it. He kicked his mount forward.

He rested the carbine on his lap, with his finger in the trigger guard, as he came into the trees. It was shadowy under their thick branches, and the ground took on a steeper slant. Above, Kindred recalled from memory, it ran into a ridge of broken rock, part of the same flatiron shield that protected the Dumont Lease. It occurred to Kindred that Roth, a stranger, wouldn't know this. There were ways to get across the shouldering ridge but if he didn't happen to hit one of them he could head up against a blind rampart, and be forced to back track and hunt again. And, Roth holding as he did only a few spare minutes' lead . . .

It was almost as though a voice had shouted in his ear, warning him. He reacted with a sharp pull at the reins that stopped the bronc in a scuffing clatter of small stones and loose dirt. He shot a searching look around. And thus, by this small margin, he missed riding straight up into the gun of the man on the bay.

The big horse stood in a gather of shadow, above and a little to Kindred's right. Motionless in saddle, Croyden Roth had his six-gun leveled, just waiting for him to come into sure range.

Now, seeing Kindred halt, he fired.

He fired too hurriedly. The bullet went wide and chewed bark from a rough-scaled fir just beyond. Kindred slewed sideward, dropping over the bronc's shoulder while he lifted the carbine for a quick answering shot. Roth's gun roared again and he felt the tiny wisp of breeze as the slug passed within inches of him. And then an empty chamber rolled up under the hammer of Croyden Roth's pistol, and at the harmless click of firing pin on used shell Roth let out a bellow of rage. His arm swung up and over in a fast arc. He hurled the useless weapon, as hard as he could throw it, at his enemy.

Kindred watched the six-shooter spin, in a dim blur of metallic shine, and bounce off the trunk of a tree. He straightened in the saddle. Suddenly there was no need to use the carbine, but he kept squinting along its barrel at the big man who sat there, empty-handed, on the back of the bay. Dimly he realized that the firing back there in the open had ended. An odd stillness had begun to settle on these hills, broken only by the wind in the firs, and by the bawling of Roth's scattered herd. It would give a crew of men a long, tough job trying to chase those fear-crazed steers out of the tall timber.

He dragged a slow breath into his lungs. 'Well, Roth,' he said as the fir branches rocked slightly around them. 'The string's run out. You made the big try and you lost. You couldn't even find the way to escape.' He waggled the barrel of the saddle gun. 'All right, big man. Come on down.'

Even from this distance he could see Roth's mouth working with the high emotion that roiled in him. Deliberately, Roth lowered his hands and shoved both thumbs behind his trousers belt.

'The hell with you,' he said. 'Come get me.'

Something was wrong about it. That kind of death-wooing defiance just didn't fit Croyden Roth. He had to have a trick in mind. Kindred hesitated, but there was only one way to find out. He kneed the bronc forward, carbine laid carefully across the crook of his left arm, the

246

sights trained on Roth.

'Come ahead!' Roth shouted across the small sounds of the approaching horse. 'Murder me with that damn thing. You been wanting a chance like this, haven't you?'

'I'm not going to murder you,' Kindred said. 'There's been killing enough. There should be another way to deal with a thing like you.'

'You talk big with a gun in your hands.' Roth sat motionless, his elbows spread, a cold sneer on his lips. 'You think you're pretty tough, Kindred. Would you want to put that saddle gun up and let me find out how tough you really are?'

'Hand to hand?' Kindred shook his head. 'No, thanks. I don't owe you a thing, Roth. You've had every chance you're going to get. Maybe I could lick you, maybe I couldn't. Frankly it doesn't matter one way or the other.' He stopped the horse, several yards still between them. 'I'm through fooling. Now move!'

'All right,' Roth said—and his right hand blurred upward, holding the large-bore derringer he'd sneaked from a hideout sewn into the waistband of his trousers.

Roth always had an ace in the hole. He'd talked, taunting his enemy, trying hard to hold his attention until the range was short enough for the little gun to take effect. It all figured, with Roth in the game, and Branch Kindred had chosen to give this big tricky gambler the

247

chance to try his trick.

With no sense of haste, with no feeling at all except a cold contempt, Kindred steadied the carbine's barrel across the palm of his spread left hand. His finger touched the trigger. The rush of powder exploding in the tube jarred his whole arm. He squinted through the spurt of muzzle smoke to see if another shot was needed.

It wasn't.

Roth's expression was one of blank astonishment. Why, even this last trick had failed . . . He swayed in the saddle. The derringer fell unfired as his hand went lax. Then, as the bay horse pranced with the terror of the carbine shot, he lost his seat in the saddle and went out of it. When he struck the needle-littered ground, he was already dead.

*　　*　　*

Earl Hazen leaned against the rough bark of a tree. He looked white, shaken, completely ill. He lifted the gun in his hand and the hand trembled. He said hoarsely, 'Can you believe it? I never even got off a shot. In all that—I just sat there on my horse and did nothing. Absolutely nothing, I was so damnably uselessly scared. What a coward!'

Kindred said, 'There's more than one kind of bravery, Hazen,' but he got no answer from the man. After a moment he turned and left

248

him.

An odd lethargy had dropped over this place and these men, in the wake of the fighting. They stood about or squatted on their heels, smoking and talking quietly or merely waiting orders, silent as their tired horses. The fires that the kerosene brands had set had pretty much burnt themselves out or been extinguished, but black smoke still drifted across the open toward a few scattered stragglers from Roth's herd. Slanting sunlight worked through the haze and picked up the grotesque, sprawled shapes of dead cattle and horses.

Other shapes, motionless under blankets, had been laid out in a silent row, not far from the place where the remnants of Croyden Roth's tough crew sat under close guard, awaiting their fate. One of those unmoving figures was the kid, Tom Grady. Kindred felt bleak as he watched Milt McCune working over him.

Tom had taken a bad one, the bullet striking him under the right arm and coursing at an angle down through his body. It had missed a lung, Milt said, but only a doctor could tell for certain what other damage it had caused. A miracle, no less, had saved Tom from flattening under the hoofs of the crazed cattle.

Yonder, Barney Weil and John Drum and the other ranch owners were waiting for him. He heard one of them sing out, 'Hey! Riders

249

comin'!' When another added, 'It's the sheriff!' a cold apprehension made Kindred's hand move toward his holster, before he remembered that it was empty.

Well, he had to settle with Johnson, sooner or later. And unless Johnson was a total fool, he wouldn't insist on making trouble. Not when he saw how things stood.

Then he spied Judy Hazen riding beside the officer, and astonishment knocked doubt from his mind and sent him striding to meet them. Judy looked pale and the sheriff grim; as they stared around at the evidence of battle. But a lot of things must have been obvious to Johnson. Instead of demanding a full explanation he said simply, 'How many got killed?'

'We lost Sid Novak and one of Spencer's men,' Kindred told him. 'I guess you'd call it lucky. Then there's some wounded. Tom Grady's the worst hurt.'

'What about Roth?'

He indicated the prisoners. 'There's what is left of his men. Roth and Benteen are dead.' Kindred added, coldly, 'Make of it what you like, Cliff. We were fighting within our rights, and nothing the law says can change that.'

The sheriff didn't answer for a moment. He scuffed a heel at the ground and he raised a hand and pawed it across his fleshy face. After that he reached into a pocket and brought out a folded piece of stiff paper.

'This reward dodger just came to the office today,' he said, and handed it down. 'They've been looking for Croyden Roth down in New Mexico because of a crooked syndicate deal he rigged. A county official who'd been taking bribe money from him broke and turned informer. They also wanted Benteen for questioning concerning a killing he may or may not have done, at Roth's orders.'

The sheriff had some trouble clearing his throat.

'So,' he went on, in a flat and toneless voice, 'I'd say you'd done everybody a favor. I—' Johnson met Kindred's eyes, and had throat trouble again. 'I was coming to you for help, Branch. Hell, I couldn't go against Roth and his killers alone, and I didn't think anybody else would lift a hand. But I'd got wind that you killed Bart Hooker last night, and escaped. I was just hoping folks at the ranch might know where I could find you—and that they'd trust me enough to tell.'

'That's why I brought him up here,' Judy put in quickly. 'I knew this would change everything.'

'It's a dirty mess all around,' Johnson said. 'Judge Gore left town this morning. Nobody knows where he's headed, but I guess he figured he was through for good in these parts. Frank Chaffee is talking pretty humble now that he knows the kind of man he got himself and the bank mixed up with. Me—' The sheriff lifted his shoulders in a tired gesture. 'Soon as this business is settled I'll turn my star over to anybody who wants to take it.'

Milt McCune declared loudly, into the stillness, 'I knowed that Roth was a phony, first second I laid eyes on the bastard. How come he was able to fool them smart ones?'

'He's stopped, anyway,' Kindred said, and folded the dodger and handed it back to the sheriff. 'That's the important thing.'

Johnson still had difficulty meeting his eyes. He shifted in the saddle, to run a look over the sullen knot of prisoners.

'What about these? What do you think should be done with them?'

'They're nothing, without Roth,' Kindred said. 'Far as I'm concerned, you can turn them loose.' He queried the group of ranchers with a look, and received their affirmative nods.

The sheriff pulled himself taller in the saddle. 'Just as you say, Brand. But they better not try to light anywhere inside *this* county!'

Kindred turned away, not caring to watch this decision carried out. There were still many things to be done. The remnants of Roth's herd, for example. His creditors in New Mexico would have first claim, and arrangements would have to be made for collecting them and driving them out of the hills. But right now he lacked the initiative to think about such matters. The last twenty-four hours had taken their toll.

He heard Judy calling his name, but he walked on pretending not to hear. This was another unsettled thing, and he would have to face it sooner or later. Later. He resolutely kept his back to her, and came to where Tom Grady lay unconscious.

Milt McCune joined him. They examined the kid's bloodless face and Kindred said, What do you think?'

'It's a close one,' the old man admitted, wagging his head. 'But he's hangin' on. I dessay I can hold him together till that doc gets here. Hope so, anyway.' Milt's big hands knotted tight, then and he raised a fist in front of him and helplessly let it fall. 'Dammit all, Branch, you wonder sometimes why things have to be—why a youngster such as him has to pay the price for the greed of scum like Croyden Roth.'

'Men have been wondering that a long time,' Kindred agreed. 'I don't reckon there'll ever be an answer.'

'Well, it'll be near morning, most like, before the doc can get here. If we can have the kid moved into the cabin, along with that other pair that's hurt, I'll be glad to stay with 'em tonight. See they get what tendin' they need, and so on.'

'I don't like to ask that of you, Milt. Not after all you've done.'

'I can handle 'em all right. There's old Sam still to be buried,' McCune reminded him.

'None of your boys'll be wantin' to miss that—
and me, I never been one for funerals. I'll be
glad to stay.'

'All right, Milt.' Kindred squeezed his
shoulders. 'That's appreciated.' He turned and
called a welcome order to his crew: 'Saddle up!
We're headin' home.'

'Branch!'

He was checking the cinch when he heard
Judy's voice, just behind him. He drew a deep
breath and came slowly around. 'You're really
not hurt, Branch?' she asked, her eyes
searching his face for something other than the
tiredness that lay there in every line. 'I was so
worried.' Impulsively her arms came up, but
she checked the movement that would have
put them around him. 'You'd rather I didn't do
that,' she said, and managed a smile. 'It's all
right. I understand.'

He regarded her, gravely, 'I'm not sure you
do, Judy. I don't know what you imagine you
feel about me,' he went on, because it had to
be said. 'But it isn't love.'

He sensed a withdrawing from his words.
'No?'

'You told me once, yourself,' Kindred
reminded her, 'a girl needs a father. You've
been groping for something ever since you
learned that you were losing Sam. I was handy,
and you turned to me to take his place.' There
was only disbelief in her still faintly smiling
face, a beginning of hurt in her eyes. Touched

254

with exasperation, he said bluntly, 'I *could* be your father, you know. I'm that much older!'

'I see.' Judy looked at her hands, twisted together in front of her. She said, in a voice that had begun to tremble, 'You don't leave me much, do you?'

'More than you think.' And he laid a hand gently on her shoulder. She tried to shrug it away but he held it there. 'You've forgotten, Judy. There's Earl—'

She stiffened.

'Wait. I know what you think of him, but he's changed some. He's trying, at least. On his own hook he talked Weil and Spencer and the others into coming here today, after I'd failed to move them. I think he's got the makings of a man in him—and a father. Only he needs your help, Judy. Maybe even more than you need him.' He added, 'Believe me, it's a wonderful thing to be needed.'

When the girl would neither answer nor look at him, Kindred shrugged and gave it up. He led his horse away, but as he stepped into the saddle he glanced back. Judy was walking slowly, hesitantly, toward the tree where Earl Hazen still stood alone. As he watched, Hazen lifted his head, and Kindred saw the hope that leaped into his face at the sight of his daughter coming toward him. This was Judy's decision, her big growing-up choice. Every doubt Kindred had had was resolved, and he knew he had been right.

Hazen could be a man. It depended on what he received from Judy—and what he gave to her.

This was enough to lift some of the tiredness from him, and as he spurred away to join his waiting crew for the ride to Anchor, Kindred was already reaching ahead in his heart. He too had made his mistakes, and he too could correct them. Gwen would be waiting down below at the ranch. This time, unlike three years ago, he would find the right words to say to her.

Somehow, he thought he already knew her answer.

We hope you have enjoyed this Large Print book. Other Chivers Press or Thorndike Press Large Print books are available at your library or directly from the publishers.

For more information about current and forthcoming titles, please call or write, without obligation, to:

Chivers Press Limited
Windsor Bridge Road
Bath BA2 3AX
England
Tel. (01225) 335336

OR

Thorndike Press
P.O. Box 159
Thorndike, Maine 04986
USA
Tel. (800) 223-2336

All our Large Print titles are designed for easy reading, and all our books are made to last.